PE/MS '03   £940

D1545697

THE MARSHAL'S DESTINY

THE MARSHAL'S DESTINY

•

C.H. Admirand

AVALON BOOKS
NEW YORK

PRINTED IN THE UNITED STATES OF AMERICA
ON ACID-FREE PAPER
BY HADDON CRAFTSMEN, BLOOMSBURG, PENNSYLVANIA

This book is dedicated to the memory of my great-grandmother, Margaret Mary Flaherty.

Chapter One

*I*ndians!

Her hand froze, clutching the heavy flap designed to keep dust from coming in the open window. Eerie high-pitched yells sent shards of fear splintering through her. Chills skittered up and down her spine.

"Close the flap!" the other passenger ordered.

But she couldn't move . . . she was in shock.

The stagecoach driver had warned it would be dangerous riding through Colorado's Indian Territory, but Margaret Mary Flaherty didn't believe him. She'd thought the tales were simply exaggerations made up by some dime store novelist. After all, these were modern, civilized times—the late 1870s.

The attack came out of nowhere. One moment, she was admiring the deep blue of the cloudless sky and endless open plain; a heartbeat later, swarms of painted

1

natives on horseback charged out of the landscape churning up a cloud of dust.

"Maggie . . . the flap!"

An odd whistling noise sounded close by, followed by a distinctive thunk. White-hot pain seared through her upper arm. She tried to wrap her arm around her and rub away the pain, but it was stuck. She couldn't move. Blessedly the pain gave way to numbness.

She heard the keening sound of a tortured cry, as if from far away. But she could only focus on one thought: She had been wrong about the threat . . . dead wrong.

The long wooden arrow shaft, a testament to her foolish decision to ignore the warnings, lay embedded in the fleshy part of her arm. She looked down at it and, for a moment, wondered how it was possible that she felt no pain. All at once, the numbness receded and excruciating pain radiated up from where the arrow pierced her flesh. Horror set in as she watched her bright-red blood flow freely from the wound, drenching the sleeve of her new blue-and-white gingham dress.

A second arrow flew in the open window, skewering the window flap to the wooden door frame. Maggie had never been so afraid in her life. She'd survived Rory's death, near-starvation at the hands of the English, and a perilous journey across the Atlantic, but she'd never in her life seen anything as terrifying as the red-skinned warriors and their deadly arrows. Surely even Cromwell himself would have been deterred by the savage people swarming ever closer to the stage.

The driver cracked his whip. Maggie could hear the man loudly cursing a blue streak, as he coaxed the last burst of energy from the exhausted team of horses. Off to the left, she thought she heard the crack of rifles being fired.

"Hang on!" the driver shouted down from above them. "Someone's coming!"

A ripple of pain snaked through her, making her shiver.

"Be still," her traveling companion ordered.

"I don't suppose 'twill be a problem," Maggie rasped. "The blasted arrow's pinned me to the seat!"

Compassion transformed the other woman's face briefly, before a grave look filled it once more. Maggie decided to ignore the look and force herself to concentrate on something—anything but the pain swirling around her.

"If it wouldn't be too much trouble," she rasped, "can ye tear a few strips off me petticoat . . . to soak up the blood?"

"No need for that," the woman answered. "I came prepared."

Maggie could feel her strength ebb as the coach hurtled across the dry-as-dust country she had wanted to adopt as her own. Might it not be wise to rethink that decision? she wondered.

Maggie watched the large, rawboned woman sitting across from her dig deep into the carpetbag she carried and produce a rolled-up length of pristine white cloth.

"Now why would ye be carrying around material for bandages?" she asked, tightly clenching her teeth, trying to keep the pain at bay with a sharply flagging will.

"Six months ago, I traveled this same route," the woman answered quietly.

"This happened before?"

The woman nodded, but offered no further explanation. Maggie sensed the other woman's reluctance to discuss the matter. Needing to talk to distract herself, she changed the subject.

"With me mind on me troubles, I forgot me manners

entirely. I'd like to thank ye, but I never asked your name."

"Annie."

"Thank ye for your kindness," she whispered. "Me father named me for his mother. I'm Margaret Mary, but ye can call me Maggie."

Just then, the coach careened wildly as one of the wheels bounced in and out of a deep rut in their path. Her weight shifted, tugging at the arrow. Biting her bottom lip, she stifled a cry of pain and tasted the coppery tang of her own blood. Darkness threatened to pull her under and consume her whole.

"It won't be long now," Annie told her, working quickly, folding the cloth into a thick wad.

Sounds of gunfire cracked nearby, and miraculously the hideous cries of the Indians started to fade away. She looked up into eyes as pale and bleak as a midwinter morn back in County Clare. While she watched, Annie placed the thick makeshift bandage around the base of the wooden shaft and hesitated.

She knew what Annie had to do. Maggie drew in a breath and nodded, bracing herself for the pain to come. A bolt of pain seared through her. It felt as if her arm were being flayed open with a cavalry sword. A moan of agony ripped from between Maggie's tightly pressed lips as Annie bore down, putting pressure on the bandage, trying to staunch the flow of blood.

"Do ye have a wee drop of English blood in ye, then?" Maggie asked, groaning.

The other woman's snort of laughter almost made Maggie smile, but the effort required far too much energy and hers was rapidly draining away.

"You've got more than enough grit to see you through the doctoring."

"Doctorin'?"

A vision of her Da lying, bleeding, on their scarred oak table flashed through her mind. She felt a bubble of panic start to form down low in her stomach.

"Are you sure you want to know?"

" 'Tis far better to know what is to come, than to worry over it."

Another memory flashed. Her mother digging the pistol ball from her Da's side while her older brother and neighbor held him down. The bubble of panic burst and began to roil.

Annie nodded, her pale gray eyes softening for the first time. "One way is to push the arrow through until the head is visible on the other side—"

Bile rushed up Maggie's throat while she listened to the rest of the grim description, no doubt soon to become a painful reality.

"—then whoever does the doctoring, chops off the arrowhead, grabs a hold of the feathered end, and yanks it back out."

It was all she could do not to disgrace herself by losing the dried beef and biscuit she'd eaten hours before. Swallowing back the foul taste in her mouth, Maggie reached down deep within herself for strength, calling upon the strong stock her Da had always bragged about.

"Well then," she managed, after swallowing hard—twice. "Since I'm skewered to the seat, I don't guess whoever does the doctorin' will have to push it through too far."

"Don't worry—" Annie's words were abruptly cut off, as the stage came to a bone-jarring halt. In the aftermath of the battle, the sudden silence was deafening.

"Anyone hurt?" a deep voice curtly demanded.

"One o' the women," the driver answered. "I heard one of 'em wail 'bout five miles back."

The door to the coach burst open, and a dark form

filled the opening, blocking out most of the mid-afternoon sunlight. Maggie tried to focus on the figure, though the loss of blood made her head swim.

"I'm not ashamed to admit it."

"Ashamed of what?" the deep voice asked, as the man grabbed the door frame and pulled himself into the confines of the coach. His considerable weight rocked the coach, causing the team of horses to pull against the traces.

Tiny dots danced behind her closed eyelids, and a low-pitched buzzing sounded in her head.

"Hold the team!"

The snorting and stamping miraculously stopped. Maggie swallowed against the lump in her throat, nearly releasing the tears she held back.

"Easy, miss."

The stranger's voice called to her on an elemental level, forcing her to ignore everything but the sound of his voice. It pulled her back from the comforting darkness to the chaos and pain.

"I may have made a wee bit o' noise when the arrow—"

The words dried up on her tongue when she looked up and saw the stranger sitting across from her. Had she died already then? Was this her guardian angel come to take her to heaven? He smiled, and her head instantly cleared. Her pain momentarily forgotten, she looked up into one of the most beautiful faces she had ever seen. The sunlight pouring in through the open door framed his head, gilding the edges of his tawny-blond hair, setting off his gorgeous eyes ... his brilliant deep-green eyes.

She watched them harden slightly, as his gaze dipped down to the arrow and back up again. The lack of softness didn't bother her; she was counting on the man's strength, not his ability to charm. Though truthfully, what held her enthralled was the intense color of his eyes, so like the rolling hills around her family's small plot of land back home.

He used his thumb to push the hat farther back on his head, the movement releasing a lock of wavy sun-kissed hair. It fell into his eyes, and he brushed it aside with a hand that was every inch as big as her brother Seamus's. And maybe then some, she thought, as he inched closer and placed his hands on his knees.

Before he could speak, Annie blurted out, "She's pinned to the seat."

He looked away from her for the first time since entering the coach. Maggie could swear she felt her control waver as she watched him nod to indicate he understood the situation. The moment he looked back, his confidence washed over her. *'Twill be all right then,* she told herself.

Watching his face for a clue as to how bad her injury really was, she saw his jaw clench and a muscle under his left eye leap twice before he ground his teeth together. The sound grated across her already frayed control. Not good, she decided, not good at all.

"I'm wonderin' if it would be easier to remove the seat—"

"Hold still," he commanded, moving so close she felt waves of heat pouring off his body.

She breathed deeply, trying to calm her racing heart, and his masculine scent enveloped her. Her head reeled as the potent combination of body-warmed leather, soap, and a hint of horse washed over her.

Her gaze swept over the breadth of his broad chest, taking in his massive shoulders. He definitely looked strong enough to pull the arrow free. She only hoped he would be gentle enough removing it from her swollen flesh.

She looked back up at his face, and his grass-green eyes immediately locked on hers.

"I have to get an idea how deeply the arrow embedded itself in the cushion." He paused, and seemed to be waiting for her to say something.

"Should I try to lean forward?" she asked, truly hoping he would not ask her to.

"Can you do that?"

Maggie silently cursed her tongue for moving before her brain could think things through. Heaven help her, she must be daft. If it hurt *not* to move, it was certain to be worse if she did.

"She's lost a lot of blood," Annie began. "I don't think—"

She watched his gaze swing over to Annie's. The look that passed between the two did not bode well at all, she thought. She shivered involuntarily, then stiffened her resolve and screwed up her courage. She could handle anything . . . she was a Flaherty!

"What do ye want me to do?"

"If you can try to lean forward, just an inch would help," he said quietly. The low rumble of his voice soothed her, like a healing balm spread across aching muscles.

"I'll give it me best," she answered honestly, "but I won't be promising I can."

The grim visage before her softened, and the man's face relaxed into a lopsided grin. A dimple formed along one side of his mouth, drawing her eyes to that point. She couldn't help but notice his strong whiskered jaw, or the dark blond mustache framing his beautifully sculpted lips. The sudden urge to trace them with her fingertips jarred her. She hadn't been tempted to look at another man, much less touch one, since she'd held her darling Rory close and he breathed his last.

"She's got a bucket of grit to spare."

"Ye say that like it's a bad thing, Annie."

As the words were leaving her lips, another wave of pain came out of nowhere, hitting her right between the eyes. She couldn't hold back a low moan of agony.

The man's jaw clenched again. All traces of his grin disappeared, making her wonder if they were linked somehow, allowing him to feel her pain. "Ready?"

She nodded and slowly eased her body toward him. Her arm felt as if it were being ripped apart and set on fire. She began to doubt her body's ability to absorb any more of the pain. Fresh blood spilled from the wound, adding a bright crimson to the already bloody bandage.

He deftly reached around behind her, slipping his fingertips beneath her. "Trust me," he said, locking gazes with her.

It wasn't his demand to trust him that decided her. No, it was the raw emotion that seemed to pour from the very depths of the man's soul. His loneliness and need called out to her, pleading with her to save him. And save him she would. Flahertys believed in fate—good or bad. Without a doubt, this man would play a part in her future. Though whether he would kill her, or save her, would depend on the man's skill at removing arrows.

Closing her eyes for a moment, she gathered her courage. When she opened them, she had to steel herself to accept the bold challenge in his gaze. Did he know he was her destiny?

"Might I be knowin' yer name?"

In a flash the naked pain and longing in his eyes was gone, replaced by a grave look of concern.

"Joshua," he said softly.

"Me name's Maggie," she rasped, "and I do."

"Do?"

"Trust ye."

She could feel the muscles in his arm go taut a second before she guessed his intention. Gritting her teeth, she silently prayed for strength.

Joshua's gaze never left hers as he jerked the arrow from the cushion, the motion pulling her flush against the wall of his broad, hard chest. His heat seared all the way through to her backbone, while blinding pain brought tears to her eyes.

"Can ye just leave the rest be till tomorrow then?" she choked out, swallowing the tears, unwilling to cry.

"I'm afraid not, infection may—"

Maggie lifted her left hand to his face, giving in to her need to touch his beautiful mouth, and swept her fingertips across the fullness of his bottom lip before weakness robbed her of what little strength remained.

He stared at her, and she watched his eyes widen, then darken to a deep forest green.

Embarrassed by her boldness, she asked, "Do ye think ye've the strength to push it through far enough so ye don't cut off me hair?"

A chuckle rumbled deep within his massive chest. She smiled, leaning against him. He was her anchor in the sea of pain threatening to swallow her whole. The comfort of his heat, and the strong muscles rippling beneath his linen shirt and leather vest, seeped slowly into her bones, relaxing her.

It had been too many years since she'd leaned against Rory, depending upon his strength to carry her through. A sudden wave of cold surprised her, making her shiver.

Belatedly, she realized Joshua had pulled away from her and was looking down into her eyes. "Trust me."

She tried for a smile, but knew she grimaced. *'Twill have to do,* she thought, nodding her agreement.

The comforting warmth of his big body deserted her as he pulled farther back. He placed a hand on top of her wounded arm, his large callused palm and blunt-tipped fingers curling around the tender flesh. It was strange—her arm looked almost dainty underneath his large hand.

He braced himself, and she could not stop the involuntary reaction as her body tensed up in response.

Joshua bit out, "Relax."

Looking up, she noticed thin streams of sweat trickling down from his temples. When he locked his jaw, she swallowed the comment poised on the tip of her tongue. It would do no good to harass the man now with her complaints. She needed his help, and he was willing. What more could she ask?

The startling green depths of Joshua's eyes hardened a split-second before his left hand squeezed her arm, while the other pushed the arrow. The gut-wrenching sob of anguish echoed all around her, but she was too lost in the pain to realize it was she who cried out. A large hand deftly swept her tangled mass of hair over her shoulder and cupped the back of her head, pulling it against his rock-hard shoulder. Her body quivered violently, reacting to the pain.

"The worst is done," he rasped.

"But not over?"

"Not quite."

"If ye miss and tear a strip off me back, I'll not be mindin'," she choked out. "Me Da always said I've a few stone to spare. Losing a bit won't matter too much."

"I won't miss," he solemnly vowed.

A grunt of exertion, followed by a draft of air passing behind her, told her he was almost finished. The arrow shaft moved inside her arm as he lopped the head off it. Her lips were so dry, she touched her tongue to them to moisten them. When she did, a groan reverberated from deep within the man who still held her protectively to his chest.

"Are ye done then?" she asked, desperate to know. Her vision had grayed with the movement of the arrow.

"One more thing," he promised.

"I'll be thanking ye now." Maggie was vaguely aware that the gray had darkened. Her area of vision seemed to be shrinking with each beat of her heart. She did not lack for courage, but she did not need to watch him pull the arrow out.

"You've a spine of steel, Maggie," he praised her, pressing his warm lips to her clammy forehead.

"And a head of granite," she whispered, closing her eyes.

She slipped into a dazed state of semi-awareness, then felt her body jerk forward, slamming into the wall of his chest. The movement forced the breath from her body as he pulled the shaft free. Numbness crept up from her toes, settling over her like a soft, warm blanket.

"Tell Seamus I tried," she whispered, as the darkness pulled her under.

Chapter Two

Joshua's thoughts were haunted by the unbearable loneliness he had glimpsed in Maggie's expressive eyes. Though he'd only seen it for a moment before it disappeared, his heart recognized a kindred spirit, someone who suffered as he did. He wondered briefly if she was the one, then shook himself from his reverie. He had too many other things more pressing at the moment, the first of which was finding a doctor to tend her wound.

With each mile they rode, his thoughts turned from the prospect of rustlers to the beautiful woman in his arms. She'd captivated him, though it had only been a few hours since he'd set foot on the stage and looked into eyes the color of cornflowers. Since that moment, his mind had been plagued with a myriad of questions. Who was she? Where was she headed? Was she going to meet family, or was she as alone in the world as he?

He dared a glance down at the semi-conscious woman

in his arms. Pain had leached the color from her petal-soft complexion until it was nearly translucent. She lay perfectly still, reminding him of the moment he'd noticed the arrow pinning her to the seat.

Chastising himself for becoming distracted by a woman he hardly knew when there was a job to be done, he focused his attention on the short trip to the town of Milford. The last few miles of the journey flew by as he held her in his arms, careful to keep pressure on the nasty wound. Though it may have been easier to keep Maggie in the coach, the road to town was deeply rutted from the weather and wooden wheels. Blaze's gait was smoother by far than any coach ride, and his horse could ride next to the road, avoiding the worst of the ruts. Maggie had lost so much blood already, he did not want to risk her losing more.

Drawing in a deep breath surrounded him with her soft feminine scent. It called to him, tantalizing him. He set his jaw and gritted his teeth. He had no time for distractions. He fought the need to inhale and draw in another breath of her sweet scent. Joshua held his breath and bit the inside of his cheek. He heaved a sigh of exasperation. It was no use—he was too tired not to give in to the need that overpowered him. Burying his face in her hair, he breathed in the luscious scent of lavender and rain.

The timing was all wrong, he told himself. There was no time to think about women, even beautiful redheads with skin the color of fresh cream with a sprinkling of freckles. He was a two-day hard ride from his destination and latest assignment. He had cattle rustlers to catch and land fraud to investigate. Any one of the cavalry detachment he tagged along with through hostile territory could have seen Maggie safely into town, allowing him to continue on to the job that awaited him.

The last week of travel had tired him out to begin with,

and stopping to rescue a damsel in distress had not been part of his plan. But he at least admitted he would not have trusted anyone else to carry Maggie into town. The thought of another man holding her in his arms chafed like a brand-new pair of Levi's after a cloudburst.

The unusual sight of a man riding into town with an unconscious woman bleeding in his arms seemed to attract attention. He glanced over his shoulder. Maybe the sight of the arrow-riddled stagecoach and Army escort following behind him attracted attention. A long line of people behind him stopped in their tracks and pointed at him.

"Can you tell me where I can find the sheriff?" A scruffy-looking man stood gawking on the boardwalk in front of Smith's Dry Goods Store.

Joshua thought he would have to ask another stranger, when the man shut his gaping mouth long enough to answer, "Three doors down on the left."

"Doctor?"

The man's gaze shifted to the inert form of the injured woman, and his eyes bugged out. The bloodstained cloth wrapped around her arm obviously had unsettled more than one passerby.

"Doc's over t' the Chicken Ranch deliverin' a baby," a tall thin man stammered.

"Chicken Ranch?" Since when did a man of medicine doctor chickens and help hatch eggs?

The thin man squinted at Joshua and smiled. "Pearl's place."

"I take it Pearl doesn't raise just chickens." Impatience simmered to a low boil. Joshua ignored the man's exaggerated wink.

"She sure don't . . . in fact—"

"Anyone else in town know anything about arrow wounds?"

"I'd be happy to help, Marshal."

Joshua looked over his shoulder and noticed a large gray-haired woman standing in the doorway of the dry goods store. She had her arms crossed beneath her bosom and was staring at the tin star on his chest.

"I'd be much obliged, ma'am."

He shifted Maggie in his arms, trying not to bang into her arm, then dismounted. His boot heels echoed across the dry boards, accompanying the swish of petticoats as he followed the woman inside.

"Taylor!" the woman called out. "Clear off the bed in the back room."

A stocky middle-aged man with thinning gray hair and wire-rimmed spectacles rushed to the front of the store.

"Ida—what on earth?"

"No time, dear," she said, looking at the young woman Joshua still held tight to his chest. "The marshal needs our help. Move those bolts of cloth off the bed," she instructed. "Then see if we still have that bit of tarpaulin left, and lay it on top of the bedspread."

She turned to Joshua. "You go along with my Taylor, while I fetch my supplies."

Joshua stood for a moment, feeling as if he'd been thrown from an irate horse. Though not a familiar feeling, it was one he had experienced and would not likely forget. The woman could fire off orders faster than General Macy.

"Ida's got a heart of gold," Taylor said, shaking his head. "And a tongue edged in steel. You'd think *she* was the one who served in the Army."

Joshua started to agree, then decided some things were best left unsaid. He nodded and followed on behind.

While Taylor worked to clear the bed and spread the

tarp, Joshua looked down at his precious burden. He could not forget the loneliness he'd seen. It echoed his own, calling to him. He brushed a wisp of auburn off her forehead and was tempted to press his lips at the bottom edge of her widow's peak, but caught himself in time. No use adding more rumors to the ones no doubt already spreading through town like wildfire.

"Marshal?"

He dragged his eyes away from Maggie, and met Taylor's solemn one. "She's lost a lot of blood."

The grim pronouncement hung in the air like a death knell. He knew from experience that her recovery could go either way. So many times, he'd been on the receiving end of an arrow or a bullet. More than once he'd dug a lead plug from his own hide. Many a time he fought wound fever lying on his bedroll out in the middle of the desert with his horse as his only company, and a bottle of red-eye whiskey the only cure for the pain.

"Ida'll know what to do."

"Step back, step back," the brusque gray-haired woman said, as she barreled into the room.

Her arms were loaded down with strips of linen, and a basket overflowing with odds and ends that looked suspiciously like sewing supplies.

"Best to do as she says," Taylor whispered.

"I heard that."

The older man shrugged his shoulders and grinned. "Now what fun would it be if you hadn't?"

Ida put her hands on her hips and frowned. "Taylor Smith—"

He walked over to his wife and placed his hands on her shoulders. "You just holler if you need my help, honey."

The starch seemed to go right out of her at her husband's words. Joshua noticed the corner of her mouth lifting before she turned and looked at him. The faint trace of a smile disappeared. She was all business when she commanded, "Tell me what happened."

"I got there after the Indians attacked."

"Great-grandmother!" Ida cried, placing a hand to her ample breast before collecting herself. She turned back to Maggie and snipped through the bandage with a small pointed pair of shears.

While she worked, deftly cleaning the area around the wound, Joshua shifted from one foot to the other, flinching every time she touched the hole in Maggie's arm.

Without lifting her head, Ida remarked, "Why don't you use that basin of water over there and wash up."

Joshua looked down at his own hands and started to object, thinking to tell her he had to leave, when he saw a tiny sliver of arrow embedded in his palm. He hadn't noticed it until now. Deftly gripping the bit of wood buried in the callused skin, he worked it free.

Blood welled up from the deep puncture wound. He touched a fingertip to the tiny pool nestled in his palm, mingling his blood with Maggie's. A surge of emotion ripped through him . . . she belonged to him. Bits and pieces of a long-forgotten tale of his great-grandmother's Scottish wedding ceremony fell into place. He shook his head. Maggie bled from an arrow wound, and he from a sliver of that same arrow, but it was not the ceremonial slice from his dirk on their arms, followed by pledges of love to each other.

"I'm going to need a hand holding her arm still while I stitch it up."

Joshua was rocked to the depths of his soul. He had not thought about his family in years. Why should he suddenly remember Meg McTavish's strange marriage ceremony?

He looked up, and noticed Mrs. Smith beckoning him

to come closer. "My Taylor's a brave man, you understand?"

Joshua nodded that he'd heard and understood, though his head still reeled, filled with ancient rites and pledges of never-ending love.

"He just can't stand the thought of a needle piercing flesh," she said with a sigh. "Best wash up—I can't do this alone."

Joshua gritted his teeth and walked back over to the basin. Of all the means available to care for a wound, a needle and thread bothered him the most.

The look in Ida's eyes didn't leave room for excuses. "Yes, ma'am."

Hands clean, shirtsleeves rolled up, Joshua turned back toward the two women. Maggie stirred when Ida poured a strong-smelling solution on the wound.

"What—?"

"Carbolic acid," she answered. "Doc keeps a supply here. More often than not, he's off delivering babies at the Ranch when there are people who really need him."

"Ranch?"

"Pearl's place." Her clipped tone ended any further questions he might have had.

"Ida?" a gravelly voice called out from the doorway.

"Doc! You're just in time," she said, squinting over at Joshua. "I don't believe the marshal was looking forward to holding this poor thing's arm still while I sewed the hole closed."

"Cleaned it out?" the doctor asked, using as few words as possible.

Joshua had the pleasure of watching Ida turn her glittering gaze on someone other than himself.

"Marshal," the doctor called out as Joshua rolled down his shirtsleeves and turned to go. "Why don't you fill me in on what happened, while I sew this young woman's wound closed."

Joshua's stomach literally flopped over at the thought of a sharp needle piercing Maggie's lovely white flesh. He'd been trying not to notice the gaping wound, pushing all thoughts of ceremonies and sharp objects from his mind, focusing instead on her toes. It didn't appear as if he'd get away without facing the sewing of the wound.

He sighed and shook his head, knowing he would not walk away when he was needed. Closing his eyes, he silently asked for strength . . . but somewhere in the middle of his prayer, he tangled up the words, asking instead for the strength to leave Maggie. The need to leave warred with the desire to stay. Desire lost.

Chapter Three

By the time he'd left the sheriff's office, he was bone-tired, hungry, and as irritable as a grizzly woken up before the last thaw melted.

At least the local law did not put up a fuss when he charged him with looking after Maggie. In fact the sheriff seemed to feel it his duty to check up on Maggie while she recovered. The Smiths had argued to keep her with them, rather than let her stay over at Doc Simpson's place. Ida had been horrified by the bachelor doctor's suggestion that he move her over to his surgery, insisting that it would not be extra work for her to care for Maggie . . . rather, it would be her pleasure.

He just wished Maggie had been able to stay awake long enough to answer some of his questions . . . heck, even one would have helped.

Time was short, given the two days that would be chewed up riding to his destination just outside of Emerson. He had to focus on the job at hand, not the feisty beauty, or the disturbing thought that they were forever linked. Two steps away from the livery stable, where Taylor had taken Blaze, thoughts of Maggie's petal-smooth skin and flame-bright hair pulled Joshua back. Like a man sleepwalking in the dead of night, he had no idea how he came to be standing again in the Smiths' back room. But the pale woman who lay sleeping on the narrow bedstead was why he stood there.

She's the one.

He reached out to touch his fingertips to her forehead, when a voice stopped him.

"Can I help you, Marshal?"

The sound of a young woman's voice brought his thoughts crashing back to the reality of his situation. He dropped his hand to his side. Maggie's reputation could be badly damaged by his presence here in her room, even though she lay injured and sleeping. He had no reason for being here, other than the simple fact that he was unable to leave. He should be miles away by now. He curled his hand into a tight fist before flexing it open. He would never be able to confess the true reason he still stood twelve inches from the side of her bed, hat in hand, heart strangely empty and aching for reasons he dare not question.

"Has she been awake yet?" His gut clenched, fearing she hadn't. He'd seen others lose less blood and remain unconscious for hours.

"She was awake earlier for a bit," the woman answered, glancing over her shoulder at Maggie's still form.

Though the woman's eyes had narrowed as she watched him, he could sense she did not fear his presence. Before he left, he had two things to accomplish. He had to make it seem as if he had a legitimate reason for being here, and he had to find out more about Seamus, the man who occupied Maggie's last conscious thoughts.

He backed away from the bed and turned to face the young woman. "I'm here on official business, Miss—?"

"Cole . . . Samantha Cole," she said, batting her eyelashes at him.

"Miss Cole, I need to ask you a few questions," he said, letting his fingertips slide back and forth over the brim of his Stetson.

She looked over at Maggie and then at the open door behind her. "I suppose that would be all right."

"Much obliged, ma'am," he said in a low voice.

His gaze slid from Miss Cole to the looking glass hanging on the wall over the washstand. He flinched at the sight of his own glittering green eyes staring back at him. The look clearly said *Back off, don't mess with me.*

"Do you know where Miss Flaherty was headed?" he asked, drawing his gaze away from the mirror and back to the young woman. Not waiting for a response, he asked, "Do you know if she was going to visit with any kinfolk?"

She shook her head no in response to both questions.

Joshua was starting to feel a gnawing tension fill his insides. He recognized the familiar feeling and chose to ignore the burning sensation. It would either go away on its own, or he'd be riding out to the Ryan spread bent over in his saddle, clutching his aching belly.

Best to leave before it got any worse. Besides, he had only one question that he really wanted to know the answer to. "Did she mention anyone named Seamus?"

He saw the woman's mouth curve into a shy smile, then look away. "As a matter of fact she did." She paused as if remembering. "She said something about sending a wire to him, then sort of drifted off to sleep."

Well, that didn't help him out a whole lot, but it was better than nothing.

"I'll be back in a few days." Shoving his hat on his head, he strode to the door. His gut continued to burn with each unanswered question. The longer he stood within the confines of the small room, the more urgent his need to get away.

"She said something about leaving town in the morning," Miss Cole called out.

That stopped him in his tracks. He turned around, shoving his hat to the back of his head with his thumb. "What did Ida have to say about that?" As if he could not guess.

Miss Cole took her time answering. Long enough to have him notice a faint blush staining her pale cheeks. She was tall and slender with pale blond ringlets that bounced every time she moved her head. After their brief conversation, he judged that to be just about every time she opened her mouth to speak.

She was pretty enough, but he didn't feel the same spontaneous connection he had with Maggie. Maybe it was the contrast between the two women. Maggie was tiny, but with a generous figure. He could still remember the way it felt to hold her against him in that moment before he removed the arrow. He remembered the way her lush curves fit perfectly to the hard planes of his own body. His head had swum with a dizziness he could not explain. At the time he attributed it to the nasty job of removing the arrow; now he was not so sure that was the cause. While he admired her figure, he had to be honest, it was her inner fire that burned so brightly within her. That and the glimpse of loneliness that he'd seen in her expressive blue eyes. She had tied him up in knots from the moment he laid eyes on her.

"She's not going anywhere," Mrs. Smith said, walking into the room, interrupting his dangerous thoughts.

He was dead tired. Why else would he continue to stand here staring down at Maggie? She was no longer his responsibility. It was time to cut loose and walk away. Besides, it wouldn't do to get careless now. He had to focus on his work. In a few weeks this job would be over, and he would either have to move on to his next assignment, or hand in the letter of resignation he'd been carrying around in his shirt pocket for the last two months. If he chose the latter, he'd need to look for a piece of land to buy up, dig roots in, and settle down. Then he could begin to look for a wife. . . .

The sound of Ida clearing her throat jarred him out of his wandering thoughts. He saw the older woman smile, before she turned toward him and promptly frowned. It was more than obvious she was put out that he was in the room. He couldn't say that he blamed her. He'd nearly keeled over the first time Doc Simpson slid the needle into Maggie's flesh. Ida had been forced to stop and find a stool for him to sit on. Besides, it wasn't proper, and if Ida Smith had told him once, she'd told him a dozen times, she would care for Maggie's reputation as well as her injury.

"Marshal," she said, striving to sound civil. Joshua figured it was like trying to drink sour milk. He'd had to once out of near-starvation years ago and could honestly imagine that his own expression then mirrored the pained look on Mrs. Smith's round face now.

"Is there anything I can do for you?" Her tone suggested she didn't think there was.

He glanced over to where Maggie lay, and then back at the stern-faced, gray-haired matron. "No, ma'am," he answered, in what he hoped was a respectful tone. "Miss Cole just finished answering my questions."

"Oh." Ida placed a hand to her breast. "I didn't realize you were here on official business."

He bit the inside of his cheek, to keep from commenting on her assumption. "I'm headed to Emerson on official business. The fact that the stagecoach Miss Annie Brown and Miss Flaherty were traveling in was attacked by hostile Indians, who had no business being so close to town, just adds another reason for my being in the area."

The older woman tilted her head to one side and slowly smiled at him. "Still feeling light-headed, Marshal?"

He smiled, acknowledging the veiled sarcasm as receiving his due. Ida would never shirk any duty that came her way, or let anyone else ignore theirs. Before he could reassure her he was fully recovered, he was interrupted.

"I hate to rush off," Miss Cole said, calling his attention to her once more, "but Mamma's waiting supper on me."

"Thank you, Samantha, dear." Ida walked with her to the door. When Samantha had gone, Ida turned back to him. "Now then, Marshal, is there anything else you'd like to ask me?"

He was bombarded with feelings he didn't quite know what to do with, and questions he had no right to ask. If he didn't know better, he'd think it was fear that caused his burning stomach to knot up, transporting him back in time to the day his parents were buried. The knot of fear in his stomach started when his neighbor had tearfully relayed the news of the carriage accident. It had started to burn watching their coffins being laid side by side.

He had run away, fear nipping at his boot heels, twelve years old and all alone. He stopped running long after dark, thankfully stumbling into Jed and Essie Slater's barn. The kind couple took him in, healing the ache in his stomach, and eventually the one in his heart. Jed was an honest man, and had made a marked difference in the young orphan's life. Joshua paid him back by working as hard as he could on the ranch and later by becoming a U.S. Marshal to help protect honest, law-abiding citizens like the Slaters.

"Well." The exasperation in her voice snapped him back to the present.

Fragmented thoughts from his childhood and young adulthood skittered around in his brain, dancing in and out of the main focus of this thoughts. Maggie.

"Has anyone come to visit Maggie?" He truly hoped whomever she was traveling to meet had come to town to meet the stage. He envisioned an older woman, not unlike Ida Smith, welcoming Maggie with open arms.

"No one. I don't think the poor thing has any relations expecting her at all."

The image his mind created, of a motherly relative embracing Maggie, blurred for a moment and disappeared, replaced with the disturbing image of Maggie being held against a tall dark-haired man. The knots in his stomach doubled up. This was the first time he had developed the fiery stomach thinking about a female. In fact, he hadn't had the problem flare up in quite a few months. Maybe it was the thought of Maggie being alone in the world. Just as he had been after his parents died. Though it might be cruel of him, he'd rather see her alone than with the bothersome image his brain had conjured up of the faceless dark-haired man.

In an effort to block out that unwelcome image, he tried to remember how it felt to hold her in his arms. Warmth flowed through him, easing the burning in his gut and filling him with a strange sense of contentment.

Granted, holding her against him had been out of necessity, and under normal circumstances he would never have been forced into such intimate contact with a woman he hardly knew, but the powerful feelings she roused could not be ignored. What he would do with those feelings, and how he would keep his mind focused, moved to the forefront of his thoughts.

Setting those thoughts aside, he was finally able to concentrate on the situation at hand. "We'll have to wait a few days until she's feeling up to answering some questions."

"But I can't help but wonder why no one came to meet her." Ida's voice trailed off into a whisper.

"Maybe she wasn't due to get off at Milford," he suggested. "There are a few more stops west of here. Someone could be waiting farther on down the line."

The very thought of someone waiting—the faceless Seamus—rankled.

"Maybe I could send a wire on to Emerson," Ida said, tapping a finger to her chin.

"You do that." Joshua nodded. "I'll keep in touch with the sheriff, just in case someone starts looking for a woman matching Maggie's description."

Ida stood quietly for a moment, as if lost in thought, then briskly smoothed her skirts and smiled at him. Obviously his cue to take his leave. "I'll be back as soon as I can." He touched the brim of his hat briefly in farewell.

Walking away from Maggie's still figure was harder than he had imagined. He clenched his jaw and strode out the door without a backward glance, onto the aging board sidewalk. More than one board creaked and groaned in protest as he pounded his full weight against them. It felt good to release some of the pent-up frustration he was feeling. He almost wished for a barroom brawl to release the rest of it.

Out of the corner of his eye, he caught a glimpse of himself in one of the storefront windows. The man reflected in the glass looked determined, purposefully walking toward the livery stable, a matched set of Colts slung low on his hips and a silver star on his chest. Unapproachable, he thought. But if his stance was part of the reason most folks were reluctant to approach him, then he reasoned it was also part of the reason he was still alive. A bit of reticence on the part of the outlaws he came in contact with while performing his job as a U.S. Marshal would help to keep him alive just a bit longer.

Though his outward appearance bespoke the confidence necessary for the job of marshal, inside his gut twisted with worry over a woman he'd do best to forget. *She probably has a sweetheart waiting for her,* he thought, unconsciously gritting his teeth, walking into the semi-dark stable building with its welcoming scent of hay and horse.

He paid the grim-faced owner and led his horse out of the corral. Swinging up into the saddle, his knee banged into the empty leather scabbard, reminding him he'd asked Taylor to leave his rifle with the sheriff after leaving his horse at the livery stable.

"One more stop, boy," he murmured, squeezing his knees against the broad strong sides of his roan. Blaze responded to the urging and moved forward.

The sheriff's office was just down the road. "Mighty fine rifle you got there, Marshal." Sheriff Roscoe reluctantly handed over the Winchester he'd been keeping for Joshua.

"It does the job."

"Been thinking 'bout buying one of them repeatin'

rifles myself," the sheriff said, with one last wishful look at the long smooth barrel.

"It saved my hide more than once," Joshua admitted. "Thanks for letting me leave it here."

"I'm surprised you'd let it out of your sight."

Joshua laughed wryly. "I didn't want to scare Mrs. Smith, arriving at her store armed to the teeth."

He noticed the sheriff's eyes settle on the pair of Colts he wore. ".38?"

".45," Joshua answered, not even trying to hide the pride in his voice.

The Peacemaker had been aptly named and earned its reputation more than once, helping him settle minor disputes and even a range war or two.

"Good luck, Marshal."

Joshua touched the brim of his hat, turned, and headed back outside. He unhitched his mount and ran a hand down the distinctive white line that ran from between Blaze's eyes all the way to the top edge of his velvety muzzle, then back up again. The familiar feel of rough horsehide beneath his hand soothed him.

He ran a hand from shoulder to fetlock on both sides of the big roan, thinking it had been a rough few days. No point in having his horse come up lame, just because he was too distracted to check his animal's hooves for tiny stones.

He checked the cinch and nodded to himself, satisfied it was secure. Sheathing his rifle, he put a hand on the saddle horn, his left foot in the stirrup, and swung up into the saddle. If he was going to make it out to the Ryan spread by tomorrow, he'd best get to it.

Mentally going over the directions he'd been given in the wire he'd received from James Ryan, he turned his horse west, blocking out all thoughts save those of the upcoming job. He had a bunch of rustlers to round up and a crooked banker suspected of land fraud. Instead of mentally reviewing the most recent wanted posters he'd studied before leaving Denver, his mind's eye captured one of a red-headed female with soft blue eyes and a sugar-sweet smile.

Chapter Four

The insistent throbbing in her shoulder, and the nauseous feeling in her stomach, woke Maggie from her injury-enforced slumber. She opened one eye. The soft light filtering in through the faded flour sack curtain did not hurt too much, so she bravely opened the other. A warm breeze blew in, billowing the curtain, letting a breath of fresh air into the tiny room.

Unfamiliar with her surroundings, she let her gaze sweep the room. The bare pine floorboards had been swept clean recently. In fact, a corn-husk broom leaned in one corner, a pile of dirt hiding behind it. Either the woman who did the sweeping had been pressed for time, or she needed to pay a bit more attention to her housekeeping. An oval looking glass hung on the wall, directly across from the bed, over a washstand that had been painted a pale green.

A tired-looking, heart-shaped face watched her with a

look of trepidation. *Poor thing's pale as flour,* Maggie thought to herself. She blinked, and the pale face blinked. For heaven's sake! It was herself she looked at. Her mind must be in quite a state to not have immediately recognized her own image in the silvered glass. Looking closely, she noticed strands of red hair hanging in her face. She lifted her right arm to brush them away, and a slashing pain ripped through her arm from elbow to shoulder. Instinctively, her left hand shot over to hold it firmly in place, while she breathed in deep gulps of air, hoping the worst of the pain would pass.

The thickness of the bandage beneath her fingertips reminded her of the hazardous ride and the arrow that had penetrated her arm. It was a very good thing she had flesh enough to spare, or else surely the arrow would have hit bone. The thought of waking up with one less arm jarred her out of the semi-dazed state she had been in.

The skin under the bandage felt tight, and she wondered if there were threads holding it together. She shook her head at herself, remembering the gaping hole in her arm; no doubt it had needed threads to bind it together. No point in worrying over what the scar would look like either, she told herself. Instead, she should concentrate on healing so she could continue her journey. She would worry about regaining the full use of her arm after she'd seen Seamus.

A wave of panic welled up from the pit of her stomach. She tried not to think about never playing the piano again, or never having the ability to knead bread dough or piecrust. She needed two arms to hold the babes she someday hoped to bear. So many things she needed to do, and she was only now realizing how grateful she should have been that she had spent the last twenty-one years all in one piece.

Needing something to take her mind off the pain in her arm, she recited her mother's recipes for apple pie and soda bread. The continued roiling in her stomach indicated it might be better to think of something other than food. She closed her eyes and dreamed of holding a babe in her arms. She curved her left arm around the dream babe, so small and needy, with sun-kissed curls and bright green eyes—

Her head snapped up, and her eyes shot open. Her reflection in the mirror made a mockery of her daydream. She had flaming red hair and bright blue eyes—just like Ma. Her brother Seamus, their Da, and even Rory, had the same bright blue eyes and thick, wavy black hair. She didn't even know anyone with grass-green eyes. . . .

"Joshua," she said softly, his name coming easily to her lips.

Now *there* was a man worth dreaming about, she thought, settling back against the soft lavender-scented pillows. The movement was uncomfortable, but not unbearable, so long as her thoughts stayed focused on the man from the stagecoach. Other than Rory Muldoon, he was the most handsome man she'd ever seen. His jaw had been chiseled and firm. His shoulders—well, maybe it was not a good idea to think about the width of them too much. Her brain was just foggy enough to make her wonder if they had been quite as wide as she'd remembered, or if the loss of blood had affected her memory.

Her hands tingled as her thoughts centered around the feel of his full sculpted bottom lip beneath her fingertips. She blushed recalling her forwardness and his startled reaction. Her head swam remembering the subtle scent of male wrapped in body-warmed leather. Her heart pounded remembering what it felt like to be enveloped in his strong muscled arms, held safe against his rock-hard chest.

She couldn't remember the last time her Da or her brother had hugged her close like that, and it had been too many years since her darling Rory had held her in his arms while they'd planned their wedding. *Rory.* Strong arms and broad shoulders. He was a big man, her Rory. She remembered the last time they'd talked of the improvements to his farm, and the two crops they would be raising. Potatoes and black-haired, blue-eyed Muldoons. His dying wish, and her solemn promise that she find another man worthy of her love, was the only thing that kept her going after his sudden illness and tragic death stole him from her life weeks before they were to wed.

Strong stock, her mother had bragged. Like her mother before her, the Ryans were made of strong stock. A head of granite was what her Da would say to that. She missed them both so much her heart ached. The pain of their deaths was still strong enough to wring a bucket of tears from her aching heart and empty soul.

"You're awake!" a gray-haired woman holding a tray called out, from where she stood framed in the doorway to the room.

Maggie's wandering mind snapped back to the present.

"Aye. This is the second time strangers have extended their kindness to me. Thank ye for taking me into your home."

Maggie watched the stern lines bracketing the woman's mouth ease. "I couldn't very well leave you to lie bleeding in the street," she huffed, as if affronted by the very idea. "I'm Ida . . . Ida Smith."

" 'Tis glad I am that ye didn't, Mrs. Smith," Maggie said softly. "I know that I have added to yer burden, and I intend to make up for that, but for now can ye tell me where I am?" She was almost afraid to ask, fearful of finding out that she was still days away from her destination—her brother's ranch—with no foreseeable way to get there in the week or so until she healed.

"You are in the town of Milford." Ida bustled into the room and set the tray down on the dresser top, the only available surface.

Maggie eyed the tray with interest. Though her stomach was still uneasy, most of the nausea had gone. She watched as Ida stirred a cup she hoped contained strong tea the way she and her Da preferred it: one sip to open the eyes, two to chase the sleep from them, and three to put a spring in your step to help you face the day.

"I've brought you what the doctor ordered," Ida said, in a voice that brooked no argument. "Weak tea and a bit of unbuttered bread with beef broth to soak it in."

Maggie's sigh must have been louder than she intended.

"Doctor's orders." This time, just a hint of a smile began to lighten Ida's dour expression.

"Does this doctor have something against feeding gravely injured patients, or just the ones with Irish blood?" Maggie had not meant to sound so surly, but her arm ached, her stomach was empty, and she still didn't know how she was going to get word to her brother.

"Doc Simpson is a good man." Ida chuckled. "For a treat, he's said you're to have bread soaked in milk for dessert."

Maggie closed her eyes and groaned out loud. She'd be a shadow of her former plump self in a week on such a stingy diet.

Ida's broad smile lifted years from her round face and added a twinkle to her eyes. "I may be persuaded to add half a spoon of blackstrap molasses to the milk, if you eat every bite of your dinner."

"I don't suppose I could convince you to change yer

mind and bring a bit of butter and jam for the bread . . .
I'd rather have the bread dry, if ye don't mind."

Ida shook her head and smiled. "I think we'll get along
just fine, Maggie, if you mind the doctor's orders and
stay put."

Maggie frowned, toying with the edge of the blanket.
"I've yet to have much success staying put," she said
slowly. "I have to send a wire to someone."

"You can worry about that later. Rest now," Ida said,
a stern note creeping into her voice.

Maggie bit her tongue. She'd almost let it slip who
she needed to send the wire to. "I have to be somewhere
by the end of the week," Maggie began.

"You have to give the stitches a chance to heal. You
are not leaving that bed until the doctor is satisfied—"

"Did he say how long before I can leave?"

"Where would you go?"

Panic had her hold back the answer, and Seamus's
warning ringing in her head. *"Tell no one who you are, or
where you're going,"* he had urged. *"Send a wire to
James Ryan when you get to Emerson. I'll meet the stage."*

"I've a sick aunt who needs me." Maggie hated to lie.

"You'll do her no good in the shape you're in."

"If the doctor—"

"Give it a few days, then we'll see what the doctor
says."

"But—"

"Doc said you were to stay put for a week."

Maggie could see that Ida's agitation was going to
skip over annoyed and go all the way to anger. She re-
gretted upsetting the woman, but it couldn't be helped.
"I can't . . . I'm sorry, but I'll be goin' by Friday."

Ida's face flushed beet-red. "Great-grandmother!" she
exclaimed, then mumbled something Maggie could not
quite catch under her breath.

Maggie didn't want to push Ida, but she had to. "If you'll just promise to help me."

Maggie watched Ida's coloring and expression return to normal, and could tell she was thinking about it. Relief washed over her. Seamus had worked too long and too hard to lose everything now. She couldn't let him down. If her instincts were right, she would not have to.

"I'll speak to the doctor," Ida said slowly, "but you'll have to promise to stay in bed for the next three days."

Maggie opened her mouth to argue, but Ida added, "I'm your only source of food, and the only hope of getting that hair washed."

Maggie felt the hot flush of embarrassment creep up her throat, all the way to the rounded tip of the widow's peak that made her face seem heart-shaped. "Ye drive a hard bargain, Ida," she said, willing to acknowledge the woman definitely knew her way around difficult people. Her mother had often despaired of Maggie ever learning to be accommodating. It was just not in her nature. It would seem that somehow Ida had sensed it as well.

"I'll promise to do what the doctor ordered, and eat broth-soaked bread, but only for a few days. I'll starve otherwise!"

"Frankly, Maggie," the older woman said, eyeing her from head to toe, "I don't think a few days on bread and broth will hurt you one bit."

Maggie began to sputter, outraged at the hint that she had enough flesh to spare losing a bit of it. It was one thing to admit to your own flaws, she thought, but quite another altogether for someone else to point them out.

"I don't believe in prettying up what's best said flat out." Ida crossed her arms under her ample bosom in a posture that was clearly meant to challenge. "Besides, you are hungry, aren't you?"

Maggie's outrage was short-lived. Ida Smith reminded her of her own mother, outspoken to the point where you'd find yourself looking for something to stuff in the dear woman's mouth, but at the same time grateful for her grand heart. She suspected that deep down, Ida hid a heart of gold.

"Maybe I could eat."

Ida pulled up a chair and held an enamelware cup out to Maggie before sitting down.

Maggie smiled. "If I behave and finish me supper, can ye add the blackstrap to the milk?"

"My dear girl, I may even be coerced into adding a whole spoon of it along with an extra slice of bread."

"Ye drive a hard bargain." Maggie smiled. "But I'm takin' it."

Her smile was reflected back at her, and she sensed a softening in Ida's initial attitude toward her. Given time, she knew she could convince Ida to help her get a message to Seamus. For now it was best to appear to acquiesce, or at the very least distract Ida from guessing her purpose for traveling to Emerson.

"Tell me, are there any eligible bachelors in Milford?"

Ida's eyes lit up at the prospect of divulging the latest gossip. She drew in a deep breath and began, "Ezra Jones is a well-propertied man, but then, so is Zeke Martin. I declare," she said, laying a hand to her ample breast, "If that Samantha Cole had half a brain in her head, she'd stop dithering about and marry poor Zeke."

Maggie sighed and held the empty cup in her lap as Ida extolled Zeke's virtues.

". . . and that house of his! So many rooms and no one to share it with. . . ."

She closed her eyes and tried to imagine a life working beside the virtuous Zeke Martin. But the only face that came to mind belonged to a certain green-eyed lawman.

Chapter Five

Joshua's eyes narrowed as he surveyed the empty yard. No sign of life moved near the ranch house. No puff of smoke rose up from the chimney. He breathed deeply, but only caught the scent of fresh-cut hay, rich damp earth, and cattle. No welcoming smell of coffee brewing, or midday meal cooking, wafted toward him on the breeze. Something was not quite right here. His sixth sense had the fine hairs on the back of his neck prickling at attention.

In a practiced move, he pulled his rifle from the leather scabbard and rested it across his thighs. No sense courting disaster, he reasoned. His instincts never lied . . . something was wrong. He reined in next to the corral by the barn and swung his foot over the top of his saddle. Before his boot could touch the ground, the metallic click of a rifle being cocked confirmed his suspicions.

"Drop your rifle and step down out of that saddle real slow," a gruff voice ordered from behind him.

Taking the order in stride, and banking on his next move being the right one, he stepped down and spun on the balls of his feet, rifle cocked, aimed, and ready to fire.

"You expecting trouble, friend?" Joshua asked, years of practice enabling him to keep his voice steady. Not a hint of the unease still skittering up and down his spine showed.

The dark-haired, rawboned man who slung the challenge at him had a rifle pointed at Joshua's heart, but lowered it a fraction as the hard look in the other man's eyes changed to one of speculation. "Trouble comes in all forms."

Joshua nodded his agreement, but didn't mirror the man's movement. He kept his rifle trained on its target. One wrong move and the hard-eyed man facing him down would be finished. As if the man sensed Joshua's intention, he raised his rifle in the air and fired two quick shots.

"How many men will answer that signal?"

"Well now, there's Reilly, Flynn, and the Murphy brothers—"

"Where's Ryan?" he asked, impatient to get on with his meeting and back to town. Sensing the other man's change in attitude toward him, he nearly pulled up on his weapon. Instead of focusing on the man facing him, thoughts of a certain redhead slipped through his mind. His concentration broke. Annoyance had him grinding out his next words. "I asked a question—where's Ryan?"

"Well now, that depends on who's wantin' to know."

The short leash on his patience had nearly run out. He watched the other man lower the butt end of his rifle to the ground and lean against it. Either the man was not too long on brains, or he obviously did not feel threatened at all by the long barrel that Joshua still aimed at the man's heart. Joshua grudgingly admitted he was beginning to respect the man.

He watched anger flicker briefly in his opponent's eyes. "Are you the lawman Ryan sent for?"

Joshua nodded, lifting the edge of his jacket to reveal the badge that declared his rank and defined his life.

"Are you open-minded?"

Joshua eyed him warily, wondering where this line of questioning was going. If this man wasn't Ryan, he was obviously a part of Ryan's inner circle. He decided to let the man finish asking whatever questions he had stored up before deciding whether to answer or not.

"Do you take things at face value, or do you dig deep?" the man asked.

Intuition had him releasing the trigger and lowering his rifle. "You'd be James Ryan," Joshua said, closing the distance between them and extending a hand. "Marshal Turner."

Joshua was not surprised by the strength in Ryan's grasp, but the grin shook him. People greeted him with a multitude of reactions: reserve, wariness, and open hostility, but pleasure . . . well, he had to admit it was a first.

"Expected you a few days ago," Ryan said.

"I got held up," he answered, not willing to go into detail. "Tell me about your operation here." He walked back over to his horse, holstering the rifle. "Then you can give me the name, or names, of any man who's made an offer to buy this place within the last six months."

Ryan opened the corral for him. Joshua led his mount inside.

"This could take some time. There's a barrel of oats in the barn; your horse looks a bit played out."

He ignored the implied question, having no trouble sidestepping it. Patting Blaze's strong neck, he ran a hand down the splotch of white between the horse's eyes.

"What do you say, boy? Hungry?"

His horse's head shook up and down, leaving no doubt that he understood the words, or at the very least, the tone of his master's voice.

"Just let me take the saddle off and rub him down."

"Take your time. If Flynn hasn't finished off the coffee, I'll heat it up."

Joshua watched Ryan's unhurried stride and wondered if the man was too trusting, or too sure of himself, to worry about turning his back on a stranger. Once he met the foreman and the ranch hands, he could decide whether or not to waste his time investigating the possibility of the rustling being an inside job.

He tossed his saddle on the top rail of the corral and threw the saddle blanket on top of it to dry off. Before he finished rubbing Blaze down, Ryan called him.

He turned in time to catch the rest of the summons. "Coffee's done . . . best come get it before Flynn sucks the pot dry."

Joshua shook his head. On his way over to the house, he slapped most of the trail dust out of his vest and pants with his hat. Ryan had taken him at his word that he was Marshal Turner. If he were in Ryan's boots, he'd sure as spit wouldn't allow a stranger free range on his ranch. He'd stick to the man like glue until his story could be verified. He still could not decide if Ryan was too trusting and easy to rustle cattle from, or if the man's instincts were dead-on, and the rustling was a large-scale operation.

Joshua carefully cradled the steaming cup of coffee in his hands, blowing on it before sipping. The strong hot brew zinged through his weary system like heat lightning jumping from cloud to cloud. It had a bite to it that he surely welcomed, as his weary body absorbed the power of the strong brew. He was well past dead tired, but had a long way to go before he could feel comfortable enough bunking down here for the night.

True to Ryan's prediction, four men showed up in answer to his summons with the rifle. Joshua spent the next few hours getting acquainted with the acreage closest to the ranch house and the men who worked it.

The information he'd gathered during the afternoon convinced him of one thing: Ryan's men were loyal to a fault. He'd have to look elsewhere for suspects. The hands were a gruff group, and they took their cue from Ryan. Once he relaxed his guard, so did they. Ryan was obviously well liked and respected by his men, confirming Joshua's initial impression of the man. It wasn't so much a relief, having his gut instincts confirmed, as a part of Joshua's investigative process. Now it was time to search out more possible suspects.

His decision to stay for supper was twofold. He hoped to pick up some additional information on what kind of boss Ryan was, and at the same time watch Ryan's men closely, hoping to pick up any inconsistencies in their character. Although he was inclined to go with his gut here and take the men at face value, there was no reason not to spend the time observing them. His time was his own until the rustlers were caught and he wired in for a new assignment—or cut loose and resigned.

"Hope you don't mind plain fare." Ryan placed a cast-iron Dutch oven on the trivet in the center of the wide oak table.

Surprised that he had let his thoughts drift off instead of paying attention, Joshua asked, "Where's the cook?"

"You're looking at them." Ryan's grin practically split his face from ear to ear.

"We all take turns," the hand named Flynn offered.

"Himself's right handy at it too," one of the Murphy brothers added, nodding toward Ryan.

"But Sean here," Ryan said, pointing to the one man who had yet to speak, "makes biscuits that'd melt in your mouth. You're lucky it was his turn to cook."

The collective sigh from the group gathered around the kitchen table was heartfelt.

"Never could resist good biscuits." Joshua helped himself to one from the dozen or so piled high on the plate being passed in front of him. He broke it open and inhaled the heavenly doughy scent. He smoothed on a thin layer of butter and watched it soak in and disappear, anticipating the flavor of it before biting into it.

"Mmmm." He did not even try to hold back the low sound of pleasure. Giving Ryan his due, he had to agree with him, the younger Murphy brother was an ace biscuit maker.

Joshua looked over at Ryan and paused, holding the other half of the biscuit poised, ready to pop into his mouth. "What?" The look on Ryan's face was speculative, that is, if Joshua could count on the man's face mirroring what he was thinking.

"I was wondering if you'd be here tomorrow when Brennan and Masterson ride in."

"That was my original plan, but now that you've given me a few leads to follow up on, I'll be getting in touch with the men who've offered to purchase this spread."

"They won't have much good to say about me," Ryan muttered.

"Any particular reason?"

Ryan smiled. "I've a way with words, and I won't be pushed around."

Joshua nodded. Nice to have that much confirmed, though he'd already surmised as much for himself. "I'll be back after I check out Johnson, Baker, and Morrison. Then I'll question Brennan and Masterson."

"Good enough," Ryan said, with a nod of his head. "You plannin' on eating all those biscuits yourself?" he demanded of Flynn.

The red-headed man smiled and pulled the plate right up against his chest, holding it there protectively. "I'm partial to Sean's cooking," he said, with a twinkle in his eye.

"More stew, Turner?"

Joshua put his fork down and shook his head. "That was some of the best grub I've had in a month of Sundays." He pushed away from the table. "Thanks for the meal."

"You turning in?" Reilly asked.

"After I make sure Blaze is bedded down for the night."

"Breakfast'll be ready at first light."

Joshua turned back and looked at the group of men still seated around the table. Four pair of eyes watched him closely, but without the initial traces of suspicion. No sense of unease tickled the hairs on the back of his neck. No underlying tension sparked in the air. He figured his actions during the day had spoken for themselves, as had theirs. Not only were they were loyal to James Ryan, but for that matter to one another as well. He'd bet there was a story behind how each one had come to work for Ryan and pledge their loyalty to him.

"I'd appreciate a meal to carry me through tomorrow. I've a lot of ground to cover before I come back."

"Marshal?"

Joshua stopped and turned back one more time.

"Do you think you'll find out who's trying to take the

ranch away from Jamie?" Flynn's question was asked in a quiet voice.

"And the rustling?" Sean added.

"I don't walk away from a job until it's done." And that pretty much summed up his life to this point. He never shied away from a job, no matter how dangerous. A body could bank on Joshua Turner to bring in his man, every time.

The look of satisfaction and relief in the eyes of the men watching him went a long way toward easing the guilt he was feeling about the handful of times his concentration slipped throughout the latter part of the day. Being surrounded by Irishmen with thick brogues had reminded him of Maggie's soft lilting voice. Flynn's red hair and freckles made it hard to forget the beautiful woman he'd left behind. He had a job to do. Until then, he'd have to wait to sort out his feelings for Maggie.

His gut feeling that she might be the woman he'd been searching for all of his life stayed with him. But now wasn't the time. A familiar saying slipped into his tired brain: *If it's meant to be, she'll be waiting for you.*

If he wanted to catch whoever was behind the rustling and the land-grabbing ploy, he'd best clear his mind of everything but the job ahead of him.

"Any word from Maggie?" James Ryan could not keep the worry for his younger sister from gnawing away at his gut. She had been due to arrive days ago. "I should have received a telegram from her by now."

"Not a word. What do you think about Turner?" Reilly asked, changing the subject.

"I think if anyone can catch the rustlers, he's our man." Ryan rubbed a hand on his chin. Concern about his sister filled his mind. She'd promised to send a wire to him as soon as she reached the last town on the route before Emerson. He was worried to distraction, berating himself yet again for not traveling back East to bring her to his ranch when their parents had died. He should have made the time. Reilly could have held things together.

Five years . . . it had been five long years since he last saw her. Once he had made the decision to head West and build a new life for himself, he couldn't wait to leave New York City behind. He rubbed a hand over his heart and grimaced. Never in his wildest imaginings would he have guessed how much it would hurt to leave his family behind.

Now they were all gone . . . only his sister remained.

"Did she say exactly when she'd be leaving New York?" Reilly asked, his brown eyes filled with concern.

Ryan shook his head.

John Reilly had never even met James's sister, but his concern was genuine. The man was loyal to the bone.

"Well then, me boy-o, best not to borrow trouble. I'm sure the little people are watchin' out for her."

Ryan placed a hand on his friend's shoulder. "Thanks." The strain of the last few months made his voice sound rough. "With all we've faced lately, the last thing I'd need is to find out is she's lying somewhere injured—"

"I'm certain she's fine," Reilly said, smiling. "If half the tales you've told about her are true, then anyone who tries to stop her from doing what she's set her mind to is bound to be in for trouble."

Ryan agreed. "She's trouble, all right. All five feet, two inches of her."

Flynn and the Murphy brothers walked over as Reilly asked, "Is her hair really redder than Flynn's?"

"What about her dimples?" Thomas, the elder Murphy, wanted to know.

"Ye've not said much about her figure," Sean added.

Ryan turned to glare at the younger Murphy. "I don't plan to . . . and I'll not have ye oglin' me sister." Ryan's anger made him forget the need to keep the thick brogue from his voice. "I'll have yer word on it, Sean."

"On my honor, James, that I won't." Sean wiped the palms of his hands on his thighs.

"See that ye don't," Ryan said over his shoulder, slamming the kitchen door open and stalking inside. The sound of the door quietly opening told him Reilly had followed him inside.

"Can you wait another week for the proof she's bringing?" Reilly asked.

"Just a few days more," he said in a gruff voice. "Emerson won't be giving me another week beyond that to back up my claim."

"But I was there when he signed that blasted piece of paper saying ye'd paid the last cent on the place." Reilly's voice sounded rough with anger.

"Aye," Ryan agreed with Reilly's words and anger. "But who'd back up our claim that the founding father of the town of Emerson was trying to steal our ranch, if I've not got the paper to prove it?"

"And that's where your sister comes in?"

Ryan nodded. "I sent her a copy of the deed, the satisfied mortgage, and my will for safekeeping. I didn't want her to have any problems claimin' the land if anything happens to me."

"She'll inherit it all?" Reilly asked.

"Half of it," Ryan said, holding the other man's gaze. He waited for the moment Reilly realized what he had not put into words, and smiled when Reilly's eyes bugged out in shock.

Reilly shook his head. "Why would ye go and do a thing that like, Jamie?"

He smiled, expecting just such a reaction from the man who'd saved his life—twice.

"Have you forgotten the stampede?"

Reilly shook his head.

"What about that back alley near the saloon outside of Denver?"

"But Jamie—"

" 'Tis done," he said quietly. "Besides, I'd not trust just anyone to watch out for my sister."

"I'd have done that regardless," Reilly countered.

"That's another reason I'm leaving half the ranch to you."

Ryan looked out the window at the barn, corrals, and fertile grazing land just beyond. He'd sweat bullets and bled, more than once, over the last few years struggling to build this ranch to the point where rustlers would risk hanging to steal from him. Ryan knew he was now worth enough that the town's namesake would lie in order to claim Ryan had defaulted on the mortgage he had paid in full. But what Emerson did not know was that Maggie was his ace in the hole. Proof was on its way.

"She's the only one who can prove our claims . . . she's got to make it in time."

A shout had Reilly moving to the back door. "She will."

Ryan watched as Reilly pushed the door open and headed over to the small frame building where the men slept. The sound of raised voices didn't bother him. His men were apt to argue at the drop of a hat, and more often than not, argued for argument's sake. *Irish to the core,* he thought with a half-smile tugging at his lips.

Alone, the light of a full moon spilling down all around him, Ryan let his worry take him. "Wherever you are, Margaret Mary," he whispered, "may you find your way here in one piece . . . before it's too late."

Joshua woke early, unable to sleep as a rough plan of action already worked itself out, waking him. The sun's rays wouldn't streak across the sky for another hour or so, but he didn't plan on hanging around long enough to witness the splendor Ryan promised was a sight to behold. He downed the last mouthful of strong coffee and handed the cup to the rancher.

"I'll be back in a day or so." With that he slipped outside.

He'd saddled Blaze earlier, so all he had to do was put his boot in the stirrup and pull himself up into the saddle. Pointing his mount west, he began the half-day's ride back to town.

"Sheriff Coltrane?"

"Who wants to know?" the gray-haired man sitting behind the battered pine desk replied without even looking up, obviously too engrossed in whatever he was reading. His chair was tilted back on two legs, with dusty boots resting on the battered desktop.

"Name's Turner."

The sharp rap of chair legs hitting the wood floor echoed in the silence that followed. The man shot to his feet and came around to the front of the desk, hand extended.

"I heard you were on your way, Marshal," the older man said.

"Then you know what I'm after," Joshua replied, gripping the man's hand firmly.

"I don't mind telling you, I've been out to the Ryan spread half a dozen times in the last six months, and I've yet to find a trace of rustlers."

"Then you don't believe there's any need to investigate?" Joshua wondered if the man had a talent for tracking, or if he spent most of his time the way he'd found him just now, with his feet up on his desk, reading.

"Ryan's lost quite a few cattle, there's no doubt about that." Sheriff Coltrane shook his head. "I'm saying those rustlers are good—real good." His pale eyes narrowed. "Their trail always ends up leading to a stream, or it dead-ends at a pile of rocks."

"Do you know anything about Ben Johnson, Jim Morrison, or Tom Baker?"

If the sheriff thought the question odd, he didn't let it show. "They each own a sizable spread a few miles outside of town. Why?"

"No reason." Joshua filed that bit of information away. He'd pull it out later, when he had the time to mull it over . . . after he'd paid each of the ranchers a visit.

"You plan on staying in town long, Marshal?"

"Long enough," Joshua answered, turning to leave.

"You plan on keeping me informed of your progress?"

"Not unless you plan on taking an active part in it," Joshua challenged, pushing his hat brim up. The reason he had been called in was the supposed lack of help from the lawman who faced him.

The man's jaw was as rigid as his posture. So he didn't like his authority or integrity questioned. Too bad. Joshua had no use for local law who spent their time ignoring what went on in their own towns, right underneath their noses . . . sometimes with their knowledge. If Coltrane was dirty, he'd soon uncover the connection. Until then, he'd reserve that judgment until he had proof.

"What else do you want to know?" The grim look on the man's face indicated his displeasure with Joshua's attitude.

"Plenty." Joshua turned back around. "Just how many businesses and ranches does Hugh Emerson own?"

The sudden silence lasted until he was just about ready

to peg Coltrane as guilty of being in Emerson's pocket and on his payroll. The sheriff's loud sigh broke the silence, but the man's next words convinced Joshua to stay.

"This might take some time," the sheriff answered, kicking a chair over to where Joshua stood.

Joshua nodded and turned the proffered chair around so that the seat faced him. He straddled it and sat down.

Coltrane grabbed a threadbare towel and an enamel-ware cup off the low shelf behind his desk, then walked over to the pot-bellied stove. Lifting the steaming pot of coffee, he walked back over to the desk and poured two cups to the brim with the thick, black brew.

Joshua watched the man's movements, and noticed the difficulty with which the older man moved, wondering if the man had taken a ball in the hip or leg. That might explain part of the reason the sheriff hadn't had much luck tracking. It took patience and stamina to keep at it until a trail could be uncovered. The strands of gray in the man's hair made him wonder if age was settling in the sheriff's bones.

The sheriff looked up and caught Joshua looking pointedly at him. "Pistol ball in the thigh, last year," he bit out. "Hurts like the devil every time the weather fixes to change."

"Are we in for a storm?" Joshua was not surprised at the prediction. He'd known more than one man who swore he could predict the severity of the weather by the intensity of the ache in old gunshot wounds. He'd even felt the gnawing ache himself a time or two in the old bullet wound in his shoulder.

"Tomorrow, maybe the day after," the sheriff answered.

Joshua nodded and lifted the cup to his lips. He'd be

heading back out to the Ryan place by then. "I need to know everything you can tell me about Hugh Emerson."

The sheriff nodded.

"Then you can fill me in on James Ryan."

Chapter Six

Maggie struggled to scoot to the edge of the bed. That much accomplished, she swung her legs over the edge and drew in a deep breath. With her good arm holding onto the bedpost, she slid to the floor and, for the first time in days, stood on her own. The wave of dizziness assaulting her almost brought her to her knees. She'd not felt this bad last night. *Must be lack of food,* she thought, grimacing. The strong will that urged her to try to stand on her own would not let her back down now.

She'd no time for weakness. She had to find Seamus's papers. She'd already spent as much time lying in bed as she intended to. She could regain her strength after she saw her brother. There was too much on her mind to worry about convincing the doctor, and the immovable Ida Smith, that she was fully recovered. It was time to leave. She needed to get word to Seamus. Though her strength of will had carried her through once before, the realization that it might not now bothered her. More than one problem besieged her. First, she felt weaker than a newborn lamb. Second, she had no idea where Ida had left the carpetbag containing the precious packet of legal papers her brother had entrusted to her. Finally, outside of promising she would not trust anyone with the true purpose of her journey, she could not help wishing Joshua—*Marshal Turner,* she mentally corrected herself—were here so that she could confide her troubles to him. Hang the consequences, and her brother's temper, should he ever find out.

Remembering the compassion and integrity she glimpsed in Joshua's bright green gaze, she wished she could ask his opinion, maybe even seek his help in delivering the papers before the allotted time was up. If he was to be her destiny, she thought, why could he not help her?

Hoping she had enough energy stored to stand on her own, she let go of the post. Gritting her teeth together, she locked her wobbly knees tight, and managed to steady herself. She needed ham, eggs, and potatoes, she grumbled to herself. Not broth and bread. Hah—it was food for invalids and sick people . . . she wasn't either. She'd only been skewered!

"If I could only find me bag," she muttered to herself.

A quick look about the small room didn't reveal anything she had not already seen from her perch up on the bed. Disgusted, she had all but given up when she decided to look behind the tallboy dresser. Using one of the knobs on the lower dresser drawers to steady herself, she knelt down and peered behind the tall dresser.

"Me bag!" she exclaimed, relief sweeping through her.

She reached in with her good arm and pulled the bag out. Hefting the heavy bag with one hand was no small feat, but somehow she managed to drag it over to the bed without tripping over the trailing hem of her night-gown. Climbing back into bed was far trickier than climbing out of it. Finally, she decided to try backing up to the bed. She leaned against her good arm and scooted back up onto it.

By the time she settled herself on the bed, a thin sheen of perspiration formed on her forehead and upper lip. "Ye may have overdone it just a wee bit," she chided herself, before digging through the pile of necessities she'd brought with her. Shoving aside her precious sheet music, Grandmother's recipes, and a satin bag of holly-hock seeds—ones her mother had cultivated from her grandmother's garden back home in County Clare—she grumbled when she reached the bottom of the bag. She still had not found the leather folio that held her brother's papers.

Rather than sort through everything she'd already shoved out of her way, she simply began to stack what she'd looked through on the bed next to the bag. A strand of hair pulled free from the lopsided braid she'd fash-ioned earlier. It tickled her nose. She blew the bright lock out of her face and continued her search.

Exhaustion nearly had her seeing double, but she per-severed until she'd emptied the bag. The sum total of her life lay in a haphazard heap next to her on the bed. A rainbow of brightly colored ribbons tangled with gar-ters. A button hook had snagged itself in her grand-mother's lacy crocheted shawl. Too tired to look closely at the rest, she pulled her knees up to her chest, and wrapped her good arm around them.

"I'm not daft," she murmured, laying her head on her knees. "I know I put it in the bottom of me bag."

With a huge sigh, suspiciously sounding of defeat, she lifted her head, deciding to try one last time. She ran a hand around the empty interior of the bag again, but this time was rewarded when the stiff piece of thin board that shaped the bottom of the bag moved. Shifting the loose piece to stand on its side, she touched the soft bottom of the bag.

The familiar feel of her father's leather folio felt cool to the touch. "Thank you!" Relief spread through her body, loosening the tightness in her chest and allowing her to draw in a deep breath.

The fact that she had not lost the papers during that wild stagecoach ride through Indian country eased her conscience and gave her renewed hope that she'd accomplish her mission.

A firm rap on the door startled her out of her semi-dazed reaction to finally finding the papers. "Who's there?" she asked, her voice wavering from exhaustion.

"Ida," the woman answered. "Are you decent?"

"Well now, that would depend on who wants to know and why." Maggie snipped, shoving the leather folio beneath her pillow. She was too tired to be nice, and had gone beyond her recovering body's strength today on what little food she'd been given. She would no doubt pay for it later.

"You have a visitor who wishes to ask a few questions," Ida said, peering in around the edge of the door. The dear woman's smile of welcome changed to a frown of concern. "I'll just tell the marshal that you are not up to receiving any visitors today." Before Maggie could answer, Ida disappeared back around the door.

"No, wait!" Maggie called out. "Don't mind me tongue," she said quickly, calling the woman back. "I'm sorry," she said, when Ida poked her head back in the room. "Me Da always said I've a tongue so sharp, it could clip a hedge."

"You look like you fell in the river and were dragged

out by your hair." Ida frowned and stood with her arms folded beneath her bosom. "I don't think you are up to speaking to the marshal."

Maggie could feel the telltale warmth of her blush rising from her throat all the way to her eyebrows. Either she was feverish, or the mere mention of the golden-haired lawman was sending her into a tizzy. Looking down at her hands, folded in her lap, she asked, "Can ye ask him to give me a few moments to make meself presentable?"

Ida hesitated, then smiled indulgently and walked over to the bed. Standing beside her, she seemed to notice the carpetbag and the haphazard pile on the bed tilting toward the floor all at once. "Whatever are you up to?"

"Nothing," Maggie answered, cramming the myriad of items back into the bag.

Comprehension lit the older woman's face, as her gaze settled on the poor excuse for a braid that Maggie had fashioned in her unruly hair.

"You should have asked for help braiding your hair," Ida said, as if she understood Maggie's predicament. "You've such lovely thick hair, it would be a trial to care for it even with both arms working."

Ida pulled the finely crocheted shawl from the pile and slipped it around Maggie's shoulders before helping put the rest of the items back inside the bag. Slipping the leather strap through the buckle, Ida fastened it and lifted the bag from the bed. She picked up a hairbrush from the top of the washstand and set about fixing Maggie's hair.

"We'll just comb out a few of the tangles and re-braid your hair," Ida said softly. "Not that the marshal will notice whether your hair is properly braided or not, but no woman should have to suffer the embarrassment of having menfolk seeing her less than her best."

If Ida thought Maggie was concerned about straightening out her appearance before she let the marshal see her, that was fine with her. Though the thought did cross her mind, the truth of the matter was she needed the time to tame her strange reaction to the news that he wanted to see her. She concentrated on breathing deeply to calm her racing heart. She was still hungry and now sure she was dizzy from lack of real food. The rhythm of the brush stroking through her hair had her chiding herself for being ungrateful.

Ida was only following the doctor's orders. Her own lack of appreciation bothered her. After all the Smiths had done for her in the last three days, she didn't feel comfortable *not* confiding in Ida. If her brother had not been so specific in his warning not to tell anyone, she would have told Ida last night. But something must be terribly wrong from him to have her promise not to trust or speak to anyone about why she had traveled all the way from New York City on her own.

Keeping her scattered thoughts and worries to herself, she sighed, focusing on the visit at hand. She'd just as soon not let the handsome marshal see her in her nightgown at all, but given the current state of her health, she'd have to settle for the blanket covering up her lower half while her grandmother's shawl wrapped around the upper.

When Ida finally finished, Maggie could swear her stomach had tied itself into half a dozen knots. Her face was beginning to grow unbearably warm and a few drops of perspiration beaded on her upper lip. She wondered if she had begun to run a fever, despite her rapid recovery.

"I'll be right back with the marshal, but I won't let him stay more than five minutes."

Ida must have noticed the flush on her face, but decided after all the trouble she went through to make Maggie presentable, a short visit would be all right.

Maggie blotted her face and lip with the edge of the shawl and tried to relax enough to calm her stomach.

"Miss Flaherty?"

The sight of his familiar broad form framed in the doorway reminded her of how wonderfully strong he was, how capable. She was struck all over again by his powerful frame and physical beauty.

The deep timbre of his voice curled around her like an embrace. For a second she reveled in it, then realized he hadn't used her given name. Now that her life was out of danger, proprieties were obviously being observed. Well, she'd not been raised in a barn; she could be proper as well.

"Marshal Turner," she said, nodding, hoping he couldn't see how uneasy his direct look made her, or that he would pick up on the hint of hurt she could not keep from her voice.

"Now then, Marshal," Ida said, pulling a chair over next to the edge of the bed. "You sit down right here next to Maggie." She practically pushed him down into the chair. "I'll be back in five minutes. The poor dear isn't up to much more than that."

"Thank you," he said, looking over his shoulder at the retreating woman's back.

"Just be sure to leave the door open and talk loudly, so I can hear if Maggie needs me."

"Is she always like that?" he asked, his fingers curling the brim of his Stetson between his huge, restless hands.

"She means well," Maggie answered. "She's tryin' to protect me reputation."

His eyes widened and a look she could not define flashed through them, but it was gone before she could figure it out. "I've come on official business." His voice sounded oddly gruff.

Somehow his reassurance that he'd only come to see her out of duty to his job bothered her. The unbidden thought that he would come to see her because he was concerned for her health had obviously been a dream. The hope that he came to see her because he could not keep away mocked her. She'd only met the man once, she reminded herself. Why she should be concerned over whether or not she'd made as deep an impression on him as he'd made on her, she had no idea. Why should she be concerned at all? Groaning inwardly, she reminded herself . . . it was destiny.

"Well then, she's got no reason to worry," Maggie said faintly, trying to keep a lid on her riotous emotions, "does she?"

Rather than answer, the marshal held her gaze, then shrugged and laid his hat on his knees.

"How can I help you?" It took all of her concentration to keep her voice steady, and she ended up looking away before he could see the longing she hoped to hide. She yearned to be held in his arms, to rest her head against his broad chest. Maggie was beyond tired and nearly desperate for a way to send word to her brother. She could not afford to let her tired state interfere with her thinking or her purpose for being in Colorado.

"I need to ask a couple of questions about your trip from back East."

He watched her with eyes a brilliant shade of green. Then the color of his eyes seemed to change, to deepen. The intensity in his gaze flashed and was gone. Maggie wondered if he felt anything for her at all. Had she hoped he might? If so, how could she find out if he continued to ignore what she thought simmered just beneath his calm exterior?

"Were you and Miss Brown the only passengers on the stage?"

Maggie was a bit confused, thinking he would want to ask her questions about the Indian attack. "Not at first."

"Do you remember any of the other passengers?" he asked hopefully.

"Aye," she said softly. "There was a very important man—" She paused, trying to recall his name. "Mr. Johnson," she said, smiling.

"Why would you say he was important?"

Maggie had a hard time thinking with Joshua looking directly at her. The intense look in his eyes lit an answering fire deep within her, making her skin go all tingly. She could feel herself grow warmer the longer he stared. "Well now." She cleared her suddenly dry throat. "I'm thinkin' it may have been the way he was dressed . . . like a man of business . . . in a dark suit and bowler hat."

He seemed satisfied with her answer, and continued to ask about other men, whose names she did not recognize.

"Time's up, Marshal!" Ida sang out, walking into the room. "Maggie! You look positively wrung out," she chastised, bustling over to the bed.

The strain of keeping her emotions under tight control had drained her. She certainly felt like a limp rag that had been banged against a rock repeatedly, then had the life squeezed out of it. Maggie nearly smiled, thinking how long it had been since she had helped her grandmother wash the family's clothing in the stream by their home. Some memories seemed to last longer than others.

"I'm all right," she said, hoping to sound convincing.

The other woman's snort of disagreement should have

been the first clue that she truly looked as bad as she felt.

"I'm sorry, Mag . . . Miss Flaherty." Marshal Turner sounded contrite, though the look in his eyes led her to believe a much stronger emotion burned just beneath his lawman's exterior. "I should not have pressed so many questions on you."

"No bother at all. I'm not sure I helped, but—"

"You've been a great help, ma'am."

His voice sounded gruff again, skittering along her spine, leaving her feeling oddly restless. His gaze held hers, his eyes changing hue once again to a deeper shade of green. He seemed to be about to ask her something.

"Marshal?" she asked, hoping to ease him through whatever he needed to ask.

He stood, moved closer to the bed, and stared down at her. Maggie felt the breath hitch in her lungs when he stared at her mouth. She waited for him to look up at her, uncertain if she was imagining things, or if his beautiful green eyes had darkened briefly with a hunger that matched her own.

The impact from the heat in his gaze sent a quiver of excitement dancing through her. Surely she had imagined the intensity behind the look; no one had looked at her like that since Rory. Certainly she'd not been interested enough to notice . . . that is, until the day before yesterday.

"Take care, Maggie love."

His whispered words were a soft caress across her aching shoulders, enveloping her with his concern. A spark of recognition reignited deep within her. It was the second time she'd felt the strong pull toward him. It was inevitable, she reasoned. He was the one.

Before she could collect her thoughts or summon the

strength to speak, he placed his Stetson on his head, tipped it to her, and was gone.

"I let him stay too long." Ida fussed with the bed-linens, smoothing and tucking them in at the foot of the bed.

"Not at all." It was the truth; she didn't mind. The more she spoke to the marshal, the more she sensed she knew him. He seemed to be honest, forthright, definitely a man of high principles. A good thing, since he'd chosen to be a lawman.

The speculative gleam in Ida's eyes almost made Maggie smile. She was more like her mother than she first thought.

"You're quite taken with him, aren't you?"

Maggie opted to ignore the smug smile that curved the other woman's lips and tried to scoot down lower in the bed. The movement jarred her injured arm, making her groan.

"I knew I shouldn't have let him stay so long," Ida said regretfully. "I just hope you don't suffer a setback." She patted Maggie's hand. "You could still develop wound fever."

"Don't worry, Ida."

Without the woman's kindness and willingness to take a total stranger into her home, Maggie had no idea where she'd be right now. Though she was already deeply in debt to Ida, she still needed to ask more of her.

"Does Milford have a telegraph office?"

Ida looked at her and nodded.

"I need to send one as soon as possible."

"I'll be happy to take care of the task for you tomorrow," Ida offered.

"You can't—I mean . . . that is, it's personal," Maggie said softly.

"You are not well enough to leave this bed," Ida said, eyes narrowed.

"I may look a bit worse for the wear, but I'm stronger than I look."

"That may be, but we'll just wait and see what the doctor thinks. Doc Simpson said he'd stop by in another hour or so. Close your eyes and try to sleep. I'll wake you when he gets here."

Two hours later, Maggie was awakened by the familiar raspy tones of Doc Simpson.

"Ah, Miss Flaherty," he said, a dour look on his drawn face. "I see you've followed my instructions and have been resting."

"That I have, Doctor," she said, coming more fully awake. "I feel so much better, I'm sure I can tolerate more than bread and broth." She grimaced at the thought of eating yet another meager meal. Used to a much heartier diet, Maggie nearly groaned aloud when the doctor didn't agree with her.

"Another two days more before you can start adding solid foods back into your diet," he said archly.

Maggie closed her eyes and nearly condemned the man to perdition for attempting to starve her. "I'll be needing to leave on the stage Friday," she said quietly.

"Out of the question," the doctor answered, as if her wishes were of no consequence whatsoever.

"I need to send a telegram then."

"I'm sure Ida can take care of that chore for you."

"But I want to go—"

"Young woman," he said slowly, narrowing his gaze at her, "you are not going anywhere until I'm certain you are out of danger of contracting wound fever."

Maggie bit the inside of her cheek to keep from blurting out what she thought of his orders. She'd find a way to send that telegram by noon tomorrow.

"Now then, Miss," he said, "let's have a look at that arm."

Chapter Seven

Hugh Emerson stood with his hands clasped behind his back, staring out the window into the street beyond. The cloud of dust that followed the progress of a farmer and his wagon toward the smithy barely warranted a second look, much less his consideration. He had far more important items on his agenda this morning.

"Mr. Emerson?"

"Ahh, Boyle." He turned his back to the window. "You have good news?" Anticipation hummed through him.

"Another twenty head last night—"

"At this rate, it will take months to make a dent in Ryan's herd! What seems to be the problem?"

The rail-thin cowboy shook his head and opened his mouth to speak, but Emerson interrupted him. "I thought I made my instructions quite clear," he said succinctly.

"The man must lose five thousand head by the end of the month!"

"But Mr. Emerson, sir—"

"Enough!" he ground out. He was running out of time. If Ryan produced the proof he claimed to have within the next two weeks, he would have to abandon all plans for taking over the Ryan spread.

"If you can't make enough cattle disappear—"

"Heck, I thought you only wanted us to rustle—"

"Keep your voice down!" Emerson had no idea why he thought he could trust a job of this magnitude to a drifter like Clay Boyle. "You have until Friday to finish the job."

"But—"

"If you can't, I'll bring in Sykes."

"He doesn't know anything about cows . . . he's a hired kil—"

"Hired gun." Emerson sat behind his mahogany desk and proceeded to shuffle through the stack of papers directly in front of him until he found the one he wanted.

"But Mr. Emerson—"

"Friday!" he said, dipping his pen in the inkwell and signing his name with a flourish. Reaching for the ink blotter, he ignored Boyle, waiting to hear the door close. A few minutes later, someone knocked.

"Enter."

His baby-faced assistant poked his head around the edge of the door. "A Mr. Sykes has answered your wire." The young man waited, hesitating in the doorway.

"Splendid." Emerson beamed. "How soon can he get here?"

"He expects to arrive on Monday's stage."

Emerson nodded that he'd heard the message before waving the young man away. He liked Sykes's style; no one would suspect a hired gun to arrive by stage. He steepled his hands and tapped his fingertips together, deep in thought. He hoped his hired gun would be able to finish the job. Time was running out.

Glancing down at the document in front of him, he focused on the beneficiary's name ... Margaret Mary Flaherty. He hoped the young woman would not be foolish enough to travel west to lay claim to the Ryan spread after its owner's untimely death.

Joshua straightened in the saddle. Every muscle in his body protested until each one felt coiled tighter than a rattlesnake ready to strike. Though he was stiff from the hours spent in the saddle, he made himself relax enough to move with the motion of his mount. Blaze immediately sensed the change and settled into an easy trot. He kept an eye on the surrounding countryside. It never paid to be careless.

Bits and pieces of recent conversations swirled around in his head while he rode. Rather than pigeonhole each bit, he let them float around while he mulled them over. He was not surprised to learn that Johnson, Morrison, and Baker had each offered to purchase the Ryan spread within the last six months. He wasn't even surprised that the offers had been below what he figured prime grazing land with a superior source of water would have been worth. There had been talk of adding another railroad spur out this way. He'd have to confirm that information. Men had been killed for a lot less than refusing to sell their land.

As far as he could see, the quickest way to make money, without actually ranching, would be to buy up a valuable spread like the Ryan place for half of what it was really worth, then turn around and sell it for twice what you paid. All three men had profitable ranches of their own, but they would stand to make a great deal of money if they could buy Ryan out at the right price.

In between thoughts of possible rustling suspects, a petite fiery-haired woman, with the biggest blue eyes he'd ever seen, kept intruding into his thoughts. She had looked so tired, he thought. Was she getting enough rest? He hoped she wouldn't succumb to wound fever.

Blaze snorted and shook his head back and forth, jarring Joshua out of his dazed thoughts. He cursed roundly, when he realized he hadn't been paying much attention to the trail ahead or his surroundings. Great way to become part of the statistics. He could envision the wire telling of it: *29-year-old U.S. Marshal shot in the line of duty. . . .*

The distant sound of gunshots echoed through the still night air. His slack fingers tightened on the reins. He squeezed his knees against his mount's sides and wheeled around to follow in the direction of the sound. More gunshots cracked just beyond the break in the trees. He spurred his horse from a fast trot to a full-out gallop.

He saw a group of mounted men in the distance. Rifle cocked, aimed and ready to fire, he closed the distance between himself and the four men riding just ahead of him. Hoping they'd listen to reason—that reason being his Winchester was a whole lot more accurate than their hand-held guns—he spurred his horse on. If not, he could draw his Peacemaker. More often than not, those ready to bend the law were amiable when his Colt was aimed right between their eyes.

He pointed the barrel of his rifle skyward and fired. The four men turned as one unit and leveled their weapons. Two aimed for his heart, another for his head. The fourth aimed at the rifle in his hand. He tamped down the feeling of uncertainty that washed over him. The eve-

ning was just light enough to make out the outlines of
the men who rode toward him.

Though he was out-gunned, he did not lower his
weapon, but instead kept it trained on the man riding in
the middle. As the group drew closer, he recognized him.

"Ryan."

"Turner." The look of surprise in Ryan's eyes changed
to one of neutral acceptance.

It was long past sundown, but there was a job to be
done and outlaws to roust out of hiding. Joshua figured
he had as much right to be out looking for rustlers on
Ryan's land as Ryan and his men had for supposedly
chasing after them. He'd have to keep his thoughts on
that score to himself. Soon enough he'd be able to see
clearly which way the wind blew. If Ryan were guilty
of rustling his own cattle, he'd trip him up sooner or
later. It had happened before; where large amounts of
money were concerned, ranchers rustling their own herds
would continue to happen.

"Who were you shooting at?" His original thought that
he was about to learn the identity of the rustlers had been
altered slightly. The men facing him must be the rest of
the hands from the Ryan place. Either their claims of
giving chase were dead on, or . . . He decided to leave
those thoughts for later.

"Rustlers were at it again. Nearly lost another twenty
head of cattle tonight," Ryan said, shaking his head.

"I don't believe we've met," a tall quiet man said in
a deep voice.

"Marshal Turner's investigating our land fraud claim,"
Ryan told the group.

Joshua pushed his Stetson further back on his head.
The uneasy feeling that had started worrying in his gut
at the sound of gunfire settled down. His instincts had
already told him these men were not dangerous. While

he mentally compared the men's faces with the dozen or so WANTED posters he had recently memorized, he followed along in their chase. Sooner or later the guilty always revealed themselves.

"*Possible* land fraud . . . I've yet to establish proof." And if that didn't get a rise out of Ryan, he would have to reconsider the possibility of the man's guilt more closely.

"Flynn," Joshua said, acknowledging the only other man he knew in the group. "The rest of you work for Ryan?"

"Aye," the three chorused in unison.

He moved his horse a few paces closer. Close enough to clearly see a glint of determination harden the tall man's features. He casually looked over at Ryan and back to the three he didn't know. The tall one in the middle would definitely not be one to cross.

"I have proof," Ryan said through clenched teeth.

"In your hands?" Joshua asked the rancher. While he studied the man, he noticed the set of Ryan's jaw, and the tiny vein that popped out on the man's left temple. Yes sir, he was agitated all right. Good. Anger was a very useful emotion. Even very crafty outlaws lost a bit of their caution when goaded into a temper.

With soft fiery curls to match.

His entire body jolted, as if he'd been standing out in the middle of nowhere and lightning had struck nearby. He let out a shaky breath and wondered where that bit of thought came from. Thankfully, no one seemed to notice his breach of concentration. That was the second time tonight his thoughts had strayed to Maggie. He could not let her cloud his mind. If he kept this up, by next week he'd be laid out in a pine box wearing his only suit.

Grinding his teeth together, he focused on the situation at hand. "Did you get a good look at them?"

Reilly shook his head. "By the time we realized what was happening, all we could do was follow behind. Ryan met up with us as we passed by the house."

"How many were there?" he asked, hoping one of the men had more information for him to go on than what the backside of the rustlers looked like.

"Five," Ryan answered, his jaw clenching, "but they'll be long gone."

Joshua picked up on the heavy hint that he was to blame for the rustlers getting away. "They won't expect us to follow along after the rifle shots," he said quietly. "Their trail ought to be easy enough to find."

"We've been close before," the tall, flinty-eyed one said.

Joshua turned toward him to speak, and the words died on his tongue. From the looks of it, the man had suffered a brutal beating recently. His one eye was swollen shut, his lip was split, and he had a livid reddish-purple line running from cheek to jaw. The man had been whipped across the face, probably with a length of rope.

Joshua made an effort to keep his voice even, and not openly wince in sympathy for the man's pain. "Happens tracking is what I do best," he said, making eye contact with the man.

"Obliged, Marshal," Ryan said quietly. "You already know Flynn and Reilly. Masterson," he said by way of introduction.

He acknowledged the men, and turned toward Masterson. "Who did it?"

Masterson grimaced, then rubbed a hand across the back of his neck. "Never saw him."

As they made their way through the open countryside, he stopped and dismounted to hunker down next to fresh tracks in the moist dirt by the stream bed. The group waited restlessly while he took his time, but he could tell they were anxious to keep moving. And that, he thought, would have been one of the many reasons not one of Ryan's men had been successful tracking down the rustlers.

"We've lost 'em," Ryan said, cursing under his breath.

Joshua could not help but smile. It didn't bother him in the slightest that the tracks seemed to disappear. In fact, he expected them to. Any outlaw worth his salt would be able to lose a whole posse of lawmen.

"We'll pick up the trail on the other side of the stream," he said confidently. He'd followed trickier quarry before. In the last fifteen years, there wasn't much he hadn't seen or heard.

The next time he held his hand up to stop the men's progress along the stream bed, they waited patiently while he got down on his haunches to examine the half a dozen or so hoofprints indicating more than one horse and rider had passed through recently. The fact that the tracks dead-ended at a washed-out section of gravelly bank just made the hunt more interesting.

"Separate and fan out," he said quietly. "I expect your rustlers have headed more toward the west, but I don't want to take any chances that they've doubled back and headed toward town."

An hour later, their quarry had been spotted. The men converged and waited while Joshua handed out instructions in hushed tones.

"There are five of them, but only one is on watch," he whispered. "The others seem to be settled in for the night."

The nod of his head indicated four men sprawled on their bedrolls next to a small campfire. "The best way to describe what I want you to do is to think of a box."

By the time he finished, the men had positioned themselves at the imaginary corners of the box he planned to shrink up and capture the rustlers inside of. Firing his rifle in the air, and then his Peacemaker, he quickly closed the gap while the others followed suit.

Ten minutes later, five outlaws lay hog-tied, facedown on their bedrolls, cursing under their breaths.

"Good plan, Marshal." Ryan's quick grin flashed across his craggy features. For a moment, Joshua was reminded of someone, but then it was gone. He let the unfinished thought slip away.

Reilly and Masterson rounded up the horses, while Flynn threw dirt on the fire and stamped it the rest of the way out.

"It would save you boys a lot of trouble later on if you'd give me the name," Joshua said, nudging the first man over onto his back.

The man spat out a thin stream of tobacco juice that hit him in the knee. Joshua looked down at the ugly brown stain and shook his head, before moving on down to the next man. He nudged the second man over onto his back and asked the same question. The response was only slightly different. The string of curses the second man hurled at him would have made his own mother faint. He still remembered bits and pieces of her now and again.

"I don't think you'll be gettin' the answer you want out of these men," Reilly said, loading up the last of the cooking supplies.

Joshua smiled to himself and gave the third man a chance to speak up. When the next two men didn't avail themselves of the opportunity either, he nudged the last man over. He said a silent prayer of thanks to his Maker and hunkered down next to the young man. This was more like it. If the peach-fuzz on the rustler's chin was any indication, the boy couldn't be any more than fifteen years old.

"Now then, son," he began, in a suprisingly even tone, "why don't you save your mama the worry of having to watch you hang." The boy's Adam's apple bobbed up and down as he visibly swallowed his fear.

"I swear, I don't know—"

"Shut your mouth, Mick," one of the others called out.

"Don't mind them," Joshua said. "They're just anxious to get acquainted with the nice piece of rope Sheriff Coltrane has waitin' for them down at the jail."

The boy's eyes grew dark and wide, while Joshua watched the reality of their situation sink in. "No mother should have to watch her boy hang," he said quietly. *And no son should have to watch his mother and father die.*

The foul epithets that followed were more than he wanted to hear. "Gag 'em," he ordered, before turning back to the boy.

"I don't know his name, I swear," the boy said, his voice cracking with emotion. "I only know we were supposed to meet him tomorrow night."

While the others were being gagged and tossed facedown over their saddles, Joshua put the boy up on his horse, propped him up, and untied his feet. "It'll be easier to ride if your legs are free," he said.

The look of uncertainty that flashed across the boy's pale thin face was almost worth the muffled sounds coming from the backs of the four rustlers' horses. "Too bad your friends aren't as smart as you, son."

"My ma needed the money," the young boy said, his voice edged with sadness. "She's awful sick, and the doc won't come back till I got enough to pay him for the last three times he came."

Joshua heard the low rough curse and turned to look at Ryan. The way Ryan watched the boy should not have been as surprising as the compassion that softened the man's hard features. But it made him wonder if all of Ryan's men had been hard-luck cases like Mick. One brief glance at the faces surrounding him was all the answer he needed. It would certainly make it easier to be loyal to a man who inspired trust with compassion and understanding.

"A son should take care of his mother," Ryan said in a gruff voice.

He thought Ryan's voice sounded strained. Had he heard regret? Ryan definitely had more to him than the gruff exterior the man allowed the rest of the world to see. *Don't we all,* he thought, pushing aside the hard memory of watching twin coffins being lowered into the ground.

Back in focus, on top of the situation, he ground out, "Stealing isn't the way to do it," he said, leading the group back over the long distance to town.

After a mile of silence, the boy whispered shamefully, "No one'll hire me."

"You look strong enough to me," Ryan said thoughtfully.

The boy hung his head so low, his chin bumped against his bony chest. The next words he mumbled were unintelligible.

"I didn't quite catch that," Joshua said, bringing his horse closer to that of the boy.

The boy lifted his head, a lone tear making a track through the dirt staining his cheek. "Pa ran off before I was born—most people don't believe he ever married my ma." He paused. "But he did. I swear!"

The men rode for a little ways in silence before Ryan asked, "Can you cook?"

"I make a mean squirrel stew," Mick offered.

Joshua smothered a grin. It had been quite a while

since he'd had squirrel . . . never could develop a fondness for it.

"You're hired," Ryan said, coming alongside them.

"You seem to be forgetting a minor detail, Ryan," Joshua said quietly. "This boy has broken the law—"

"Not if no one remembers seeing him among that group of rustlers," Ryan said, nosing his mount until he was directly in front of Joshua, blocking his way.

"We've never seen him before, men," Ryan said quietly. "Have we?"

As if they were a trained fighting unit, the men were instantly beside Ryan, adding their voices to his own.

"Never seen the boy before."

"He just wandered by the ranch one mornin' . . ."

"He'd been beaten . . ."

"Out of his head for two days . . ."

"All right," Joshua said, considering the ramifications of hauling in the four rustlers and letting the boy go free.

"I may be willing to let you have custody of him, if he can tell us everything he knows about tomorrow night's meeting." Joshua's gut told him, without a doubt, that Ryan would accept whatever terms he offered to keep the boy from spending any time behind bars.

He admired the man for trying to do what he, as a lawman, could not—circumvent the law to protect a victim of circumstances beyond his control.

"Done," the big man answered, then turned toward the boy. "What's your full name?"

"Michael," the boy said quietly. "Michael O'Toole."

The surprised exclamations and welcome that followed convinced Joshua the boy would be well taken care of and watched closely at the same time.

"What about my ma?" Mick asked, hope stealing into his voice.

"I'll send a wagon into town at sunup," Ryan promised.

"Let's get these men settled in nice and cozy over at the jail." Joshua felt as if a weight had been lifted from his weary body. Once they tracked down who was behind the rustling, half his job would be over. He had a definite plan in mind for how he would be spending his time.

"I'm sure the sheriff can wait to talk to Mick. Why don't you and Masterson head out to the ranch. Reilly and Flynn can come with me."

"Done," Ryan answered. "We'll settle in, and Mick'll have breakfast ready for you when you return. Won't you?" he asked, turning toward the would-be rustler who rode between them.

After a long silence, Mick let out a long breath. "My ma taught me to make scones," he offered.

The hoots of approval let Joshua know all would be well with the boy. Mick might have started to wander down the wrong path, but like himself, a strong man was waiting there to redirect Mick's feet onto the right road. It had made all the difference in his life, he thought. And if he was right about James Ryan, and he didn't doubt he was, it would be for Mick too.

Chapter Eight

She had to send the telegram today. Restlessness was making her irritable when she needed to be agreeable, or else she'd never convince Ida to let her out of bed before Doc Simpson gave his approval.

Her arm was still stiff, but she'd gotten used to working around that. She was thankful for her strong constitution, unable to believe she'd regained most of her strength even though the doctor tried to starve her. She shuddered to think of subsisting on bread and broth for the last three days. Today was the first time she had been allowed to eat a normal diet, and she was more than ready to get out of bed and prove she was recovered.

"Maggie," Ida called out, before coming to stand in the doorway. Her gaze swept up and down Maggie's form, a slight frown furrowing between her graying brows. "I suppose you think because you've dressed yourself that I should let you stay out of bed."

"If ye don't, I won't be responsible for me actions," Maggie said, gritting her teeth and preparing to argue.

A hint of a smile curved the older woman's mouth until it tilted up on one side. Ida cleared her throat. "Well, then . . ."

"Well, then . . ." Maggie echoed hopefully, smoothing the front of her floral-sprigged cotton dress. It was a cream-colored dress with tiny blue flowers dotted across it. She'd made it just a few weeks before she received Seamus's wire that he needed her. Though she'd left New York a full week ahead of schedule, she was quickly running out of time. She had to convince Ida she was fine. She had to send that wire today.

"Ida," she said, rising up from where she sat in the ladder-back chair with minimal difficulty. "I'm fine," she said quietly.

"I can see that you think you are," the other woman said, coming to stand in front of her. "Here, let me help you with your hair."

The two women were silent while Ida finished pinning the coil of heavy red hair at the nape of Maggie's neck. One look in the looking glass Ida held for her and she nodded. "I could not have done it without ye," she said softly, turning to face her. "I have so much to thank ye for, Ida."

The look that came into the other woman's eyes clearly showed the concern and caring the two had developed for each other in the last few days since Maggie had been carried unconscious into the Smiths' back room. Ida sniffed and patted the braided coil at the back of her own head. "Well now, it was only fitting—"

"Not everyone would have been willing to take in a complete stranger, prepared to have to care for them," Maggie said, knowing the gratitude she felt could not be hidden. Her Da always told her he knew what she was thinking a moment before she did—all he had to do was look at her expression. Her heart clenched in her breast. She missed him; the ache was still just as raw as it had been five years ago.

"Now that I'm feeling more meself, I need to send off a wire."

"I can—"

"Ida, ye are a dear sweet woman," Maggie said slowly, "but I need to do this meself. Please don't ask me to explain," she rasped. "I truly would if I could."

"I'll be back with Doc Simpson," Ida said quietly. "If he changes his mind, then I will too."

"Wonderful," Maggie muttered.

"Maggie!" At the sound of her name on Samantha Cole's lips, she nearly groaned aloud. Ida hadn't trusted her after all. She sent Samantha to keep an eye on her, and to make certain she didn't leave the first chance she got. Well, that had been her plan, but really the fact that Ida guessed her intentions did bother her. Well, at least Samantha should not be as much of a problem as slipping by Ida's guard would be.

"You just can't leave!"

Maggie turned her back on Samantha and checked her own reflection in the looking glass. The pathetic-looking creature that stared back at her had purple smudges beneath her eyes and skin the color of watered-down milk. She cringed, thinking she looked more like a wrung-out rag that someone had used to wash the floor with, than a flesh-and-blood woman in her prime. Well, maybe just a wee bit past her prime, but not totally beyond all hope yet.

"Ida will skin me alive," Samantha protested. "She made me promise not to let you out of my sight."

"Well then, if ye close yer eyes now, ye won't be havin' to lie about seein' me leave."

"Maggie, be reasonable. You've lost so much blood."

The plea in Samantha's eyes was not lost on her, but what the young woman did not understand, Maggie could not tell her. It was urgent that she get a message to her brother. Nothing, short of the devil dancing upon her grave, was going to stop her.

A quick glance satisfied Maggie that the papers she'd hidden beneath the mattress would not be disturbed. For good measure, she pretended to drop her linen handkerchief so she could look at the bottom edge of the bed without being too conspicuous while picking it up. *Perfect,* she thought. Nothing was out of place. Her hiding place was still secure.

As she straightened up, the floor started to sway, and the room started to spin. *You're not dizzy,* she told herself, *just tired.*

"Maggie, you've gone pale as wax."

"Well now, with all the freckles I have across me nose, I can't imagine how you could say that."

Maggie's attempt at levity distracted Ida's young friend, allowing Maggie to draw in a few steadying breaths. Once the floor stopped moving, her equilibrium returned.

"Ida said—"

"Aye, ye've told me more than once what Ida said," Maggie said quietly. "I'll be back before Ida knows I'm gone," she said from the doorway.

The moment she stepped onto the boardwalk, Maggie had the uncomfortable feeling she was being observed. A quick look over her shoulder made her head swim, but relieved her initial worry that Samantha had followed after her.

According to Ida's husband, the telegraph office was

at the far end of the street, across from the bank. She hurried off in that direction. The first time a stranger passed by, she felt the heat of the woman's stare. Maggie looked down to make sure she had not missed any buttons.

All fastened.

When she looked back at the woman, the bit of walkway was empty.

By the time she had passed by four storefronts, three more women had passed by, a similar reaction occurring each time. Surely it was no crime to be walking about without an escort. Wasn't it? Wondering if perhaps the good people of Milford had never seen a red-headed woman before, she didn't see the dip in the boardwalk. Flinging her hands out, trying to catch herself before she pitched forward onto her face, Maggie was amazed to find herself suddenly weightless.

"Easy, miss," a deep voice warned close to her ear.

She looked up. The reason for the weightlessness stood a whole head taller than her brother, with hair white as snow.

"Thank you," she managed. "I must not have been minding me step."

The weathered planes of the man's face crinkled up as he broke into a broad smile. "You'd be welcome, lass," he said, setting her back on her feet.

At his words, Maggie's face lit up with delight. "Yer from back home?"

He shook his shaggy white head. "My wife was." The lines in his kind face softened from pleasure into sadness.

Their eyes met and held, as understanding flashed between them. She recognized the look in his eyes; the man's pain was still too fresh. *'Tis too soon for him to speak of her,* she thought. She'd been like that with her parents.

"I'm sorry for yer loss."

He nodded before hurrying across the street. Dust swirled out from under his boots, reminding her of the dry-as-dust road she'd been traveling when the Indians attacked. She shuddered before she was able to put those thoughts in the back of her mind and focus instead on the message she would send to her brother via James Ryan.

It was simple:

Delayed . . . STOP . . . have what you need . . . STOP . . . will arrive by stage Friday . . . STOP

Fifteen minutes later, Maggie stepped back out onto the boardwalk and headed back to the Smiths' store. A wave of heat washed over her. Far too warm, she tugged at the high collar of her dress, hoping to let in a breath of cool evening air. With each step, her feet dragged and the darkness seemed to be closing in around her.

"Let me help you."

Maggie turned toward the throaty voice and shook her head to clear it. The vision in front of her could not be real. She blinked, but the raven-haired woman dressed in pale-gray silk still sat perched upon the luxurious leather seat of a shiny black phaeton. Her tiny gloved hand held the reins to an enormous gray horse stomping restlessly in place.

Maggie had never seen such a beautiful sight in her life. New York had been full of wealthy women, but none could quite compare with the lovely lady offering to help her.

"Are ye offerin' to help me?" she asked, looking around to make certain there was no one else in greater need.

"You look dead on your feet. May I offer you a ride?"

Maggie collected herself enough to nod, grab hold of the side of the carriage, and pull herself up into it. "I'm not quite meself lately, thank ye."

"You're not from around here, are you?" The woman tilted her head to one side and looked Maggie over.

"I'm just passing through," Maggie said, shifting uncomfortably on the seat. She knew she looked a wreck, especially when compared to the beautiful woman seated beside her.

"My name's Luann," the woman offered, extending a gloved hand toward Maggie.

Maggie smiled, taking Luann's hand in her own and squeezing it before letting go. " 'Tis glad I am that ye stopped by. I was starting to wonder if I would make it back to the Smiths."

"The Dry Goods Store?"

"Aye," Maggie said slowly. "I've been staying with them for a few days."

Luann's hands deftly snapped the reins, setting the sleek carriage in motion. "How long do you plan to stay on in Milford?"

"I'll be gone by Friday, on the mornin' stage."

Luann sighed softly. "I knew it was too good to be true."

"What?" Maggie asked, caught by the woman's wistful tone.

"Since you won't be staying, I may as well tell you. I don't have many friends in town."

"Are ye new here yourself, then?" Maggie asked.

Luann shook her head. "Been here nigh on ten years this fall."

"Then why—"

"Margaret Mary Flaherty!"

Maggie's head snapped around at the shrill sound of

Ida Smith calling her name. Her given name—how on earth did Ida know her full name?

"I'm sorry," Luann said softly. "It would have been nice talking to you, Maggie."

Ida stared at the other woman. If looks could kill, Maggie would swear Luann would be six feet under. Maggie let Ida help her out of the carriage, but stopped when Ida would have continued dragging her into the store.

"Thank ye for yer kindness, Luann," she called out. "You're a fine woman."

"Do you know who that was?" Ida hissed under her breath, watching the carriage roll away.

"Aye, she said her name was Luann."

"That is the owner of the Chicken Ranch!"

Maggie turned to stare at the older woman. Lines of frustration furrowed her brow and bracketed her mouth. "She must do very well raisin' chickens," she said thoughtfully. "That dress was made of pure silk."

Ida mumbled something under her breath about eggs and innocent young women, but that was all Maggie could decipher.

"Do you sell her eggs in your store?" she wanted to know.

Ida pulled her inside the front door and slammed it shut. Putting her hands on her hips, she rounded on Maggie and spat out, "That woman runs Pearl's place!"

"I thought you said she ran a chicken farm."

"Ranch! The Chicken Ranch."

"Well then, what's Pearl's place?"

"Ida," a deep voice said from the darkened hallway, "do you really think you should be talking to such an innocent young thing like Maggie about Pearl?"

"Taylor Smith! Do you know who just dropped Maggie off in front of our store?"

"Sheriff Roscoe?"

"That man couldn't find his way out of his own front door!"

"I don't see why ye won't tell me what Pearl's place is," Maggie said to Ida before turning to face Taylor. "Luann must be doing quite well for herself if she owns a chicken ranch and Pearl's place. Is it a saloon, then?"

"Best tell her, Ida."

Maggie caught the solemn note in the older man's voice. He almost sounded sad.

"Pearl—that is, Luann—hires poor young things off the street and—"

"What Ida is trying to say," Taylor said gently, helping Maggie to a chair near the back of the store, "is that Pearl's place hires women who entertain men."

Understanding dawned, but no condemnation followed. Maggie had learned early in life that she who would be the first to cast stones had better be certain she had no black spots on her own soul. Besides, who was she to judge another? "Luann stopped to help me," she said quietly. "She was the only woman today who didn't look right through me as if I wasn't there."

"We will get back to the topic of why you are out of bed in a moment," Ida bit out. "First, I want to know what was so all-fired important that you'd risk a relapse or possibly wound fever by traipsing around town all by yourself!"

"Do all the women in Milford go about with an escort?"

"Well, of course not. It's just that—"

Ida's words died at the direct look Maggie gave her. "Just what?"

"Well, how you came to us," Ida finished in a brusque tone.

"And how was that?"

"Don't try to pretty it up, Ida. Best to tell her straight," Taylor advised.

"In the arms of Marshal Turner."

"I thought the stage . . ." She let her words trail off. This was something else to ponder. What could the marshal have been thinking to carry her all the way from the ambush site? Hadn't someone mentioned to her that it had happened a few miles outside of town?

"The marshal was worried that the ride into town over the deeply rutted road would jar your wound and reopen it." Ida's intent look unnerved her. "He was very worried about further injuring you."

"Well," Maggie said, clearing her throat. She tried to still the butterflies fluttering about in her belly, but it was no use. Just the thought of being carried about like that made her knees weak and her heart light.

"But I still don't understand why that would bother the women—"

"They're just acting persnickety," Taylor said, interrupting. "Why didn't you wait?"

"I had a feelin' the doctor wouldn't let me go."

"Ida," Taylor said quietly, "why don't you see about something for Maggie to eat."

"There might be some cold fried chicken. . . ."

"Thank you," Maggie said softly. As the older woman swept past her, Maggie reached out to grasp her hand. "I don't mean to cause ye trouble. I'm more than grateful for yer kindness these past few days. But there are things that I can't tell ye," she said, looking up at Ida. " 'Tisn't safe. I'm not deliberately throwin' yer hospitality in yer face."

"There now, Maggie," Taylor said, squatting down beside her chair once his wife disappeared. "My Ida is so used to running things, she just gets herself in a dither when people don't willingly fall in with what she wants them to do."

Tears stung the back of Maggie's eyes and a lump of emotion clogged her throat. She struggled to speak. "I've not had anyone to answer to for these past few months," she said softly. "I've only just realized how much I've missed it."

"All set, Taylor," Ida called out from the kitchen. As she walked back toward them, she wiped her hands on a towel and waited by the stool Maggie still sat on.

"I think a shot of whiskey is in order." Taylor headed down the hall toward the kitchen.

"We'll be right behind you, dear," Ida called out.

"Maggie, I—"

"Ida—"

They both started to speak at the same time, then fell silent waiting for the other to continue. When it was obvious that Ida was waiting for her to speak, Maggie continued, "Me mother died four months ago . . . me Da's been gone five years now."

"You poor dear." Ida patted Maggie's hand.

"I've traveled across the Atlantic Ocean to make a new life after Rory . . ." Maggie's throat closed completely thinking of him. She shook her head, willing herself not to cry. She succeeded, but was unable to speak past the constriction in her throat.

Ida drew Maggie to her feet and held her close. Enveloped in Ida's ample embrace, Maggie was reminded of simpler times, when a hug was all it took to make the hurt go away. But all the hugs in the world could not bring her parents or Rory back. She sniffed back the rest of the tears that threatened to fall and hugged Ida hard. Then she drew away.

"You're a wonderful woman. I would not hurt ye for the world. But there are things that I must do," Maggie said quietly. "I cannot go back on my word. I've promises to keep."

Ida's gaze was penetrating. Finally, she nodded her head and took Maggie by the arm. "Let's go find Taylor. Then you can tell me where you need to go. We'll see that you get there."

Walking into the kitchen, Maggie felt her eyes fill with tears. "I've got to be on the stage to Emerson Friday morning."

Taylor pulled out a chair for Maggie, then for his wife. He poured two fingers of a deep amber whiskey into a short squat glass and handed it to Maggie. "Drink up," he ordered. Pouring two more glasses, he bid Ida to do the same.

One sip and Maggie was transported back to her family's kitchen back home in Ireland. She closed her eyes and breathed deeply. She could just imagine the faint odor of a peat fire filling her nostrils, surrounding her with a feeling of welcome.

"A man by the name of Reilly traded this bottle for some supplies a few years back."

Maggie looked at the gray-haired man who stood back from the table, drink in hand and a smile on his face. "Did ye know then he traded ye some of the finest Irish whiskey in the world?"

Taylor shook his head and grinned. "No, but he did ask that we share one drink before he left."

"Smart man, that Reilly," Maggie said, taking another sip.

"I heard he's working for a man named Ryan over near Emerson."

"Ryan?" Maggie whispered. That was the name of the man she'd sent the telegram to. The man who was to help her get in touch with her brother.

"James Ryan owns one of the largest cattle ranches near Emerson," Ida offered.

"Does he now?"

"I heard he's having trouble with rustlers," Taylor said, his mouth set in a grim line.

"Rustlers?" Maggie asked, unsure what the word meant.

"Cattle thieves," Ida clarified.

Maggie took another few sips of her drink and wondered why she hadn't thought to bring some of the Irish with her from New York. Her Da always swore it could cure anything the devil could plague man with.

"I wonder if that was where the marshal was headed," Ida said slowly.

Joshua. An image of clear green eyes and sun-kissed hair filled her. There was no denying the attraction; she had been drawn to him from the moment he stepped onto the stagecoach. In the past three days, thoughts of him distracted her at the oddest moments.

Now that she knew he had ridden all the way to town holding her in his arms, she understood the look she saw reflected in his lovely green eyes. Remembering the feeling of safety she'd felt held close in his arms brought with it a shock of awareness. The broad width of his shoulders and the rock-hard muscles of his chest had been a comfort, but had also ignited a tiny flicker of passion that had continued to smolder and grow in intensity.

If she had to say what attracted her the most, it would have to be his inner strength and character that had drawn her to him, that and the bone-deep loneliness in his brilliant green gaze. Though he had ridden away before she could thank him, she knew she would see him again . . . it was fate.

"Marshal Turner?" she managed to ask.

"A fine-looking man."

Maggie could feel Ida's gaze on her, but she didn't look over at her. The possibility that he would be near enough to enlist his strength and calm reasoning to help her brother, had her mind racing. Maybe she could get word to him somehow.

"I was a colonel in the Regular Army," Taylor said. "Back in '69, I was with the 5th Cavalry under General Carr in the Battle of Summit Springs. There wasn't any confrontation that I couldn't handle—be it Sioux, Cheyenne, or Lakota—although there was a time there when Tall Bull nearly gutted me that I wondered if I'd see my sweet Ida again."

Taylor cleared his throat and continued, "The point I'm trying to make, Maggie, is that whatever trouble you are in, I can keep you safe."

"It's not just meself—" Maggie whispered.

She searched her heart and decided she had to trust someone on the outside chance she did not make it to Emerson. So far the odds seemed to be in favor of the worst possible thing going wrong at precisely the wrong moment. If she thought about it, she could say the same for every important moment in her life.

A week before she and Rory were to wed, he died in her arms. Two days before her family were to sail across the Atlantic, her father met with the wrong end of an English rifle. He never regained his full strength and died a month after they landed in New York Harbor.

Now, days away from delivering Seamus's important papers, she had the bad feeling that she would never finish the journey. For her brother's sake, someone else must know about the papers she carried, and the reason for her journey.

"Me brother Seamus entrusted a copy of his deed and paid mortgage into me care," she said slowly. "For some reason, he needs the copies in his hands by the middle of next week, or else the bank will take his ranch! He's worked too long and hard for me to let that happen now."

Taylor and Ida waited patiently for her to continue, with identical looks of grave concern etched across their brows. She briefly wondered if the longer a person was married the more they began to take on characteristics of their spouse, and think similar thoughts. She only just now realized that her parents had not been the only ones to act that way.

"Ye must not let anyone else know about me mission," she warned. "I think me brother is afraid I'll not make it in time with the proof he needs."

"Why don't you show us the paperwork," Taylor said.

Maggie watched him take off his glasses and clean the lenses with the pristine white linen handkerchief he always kept in his back left trouser pocket. While she followed the sweep of his strong fingers across the lenses, an idea started to form.

"Could we have someone witness that I've shown the papers to ye?"

"We'll go one step further," Taylor advised. "We'll have Jeremiah Johnson over at the Land Management Office draw up a legal paper attesting to the fact that your brother's papers do in fact exist and that Ida, Jeremiah, and myself have all read the papers and will act as witnesses."

"Not that we think we'll need to use the papers, mind you," Ida added.

"Just in case. As a precaution," Taylor said solemnly.

"Aye," Maggie agreed. "Hopefully the stage ride to Emerson will be uneventful."

"Have you the money for a ticket?" Taylor wanted to know.

"I've already bought and paid for the fare all the way

to Emerson," Maggie answered. "Ye don't think they'd make me pay again, do ye?" She'd have to go to the bank once she reached Emerson and have money wired from her bank in New York. She intended to repay her brother for the money he'd sent over the last few years. She knew he needed it, but must have felt obligated to send it to her and her mother. Her dear mother had insisted they only use what they needed and put the rest in the bank for Seamus. Maggie had wholeheartedly agreed.

"No. The Indian attack was unforeseen. The stage company should honor your ticket," Taylor added. "They knew you were injured during the attack and could not continue your journey right away. And if they've forgotten, we'll remind them."

"Well then," Maggie said brightly. Her burden felt lighter. "I'll go and pack me things."

She rose from the chair and turned to go, but thought of one more thing she needed to tell the Smiths. She grabbed a hold of the top rung on the ladder-back chair. "If anything should happen to me," she said, her voice tight with emotion, "send a wire to Seamus Flaherty at James Ryan's ranch. He's the only man me brother trusts."

"Don't you fret, dear," Ida said, coming to stand beside her. "This time tomorrow, you'll be on your way to Emerson."

"Lord willing," she prayed.

"And the creek don't rise," Taylor added.

Chapter Nine

Disbelief speared through Hugh while rage simmered inside him, threatening to boil over. Instead of giving in to his anger, he very carefully smoothed the crimped edges of the telegram, where his fingers had clenched it, until it lay flat on his desk.

He had to think.

If the Irishwoman somehow managed to get on board the stage bound for his town, all his plans for the future of Emerson would be but ashes left blowing in the wind. The railroad would officially be sending surveyors and engineers out in a few months to scout out a location. He had paid dearly to find out in advance what route would be used. He gambled on his informant's having the correct information. The land he'd started to acquire last year would soon be a beehive of industry, once the railroad moved in and started to lay tracks.

He had started planning this scheme ever since the

97

Kansas Pacific Railroad had connected Kansas City with Denver nearly ten years ago. Rumors had developed into fact about six months ago. The prospect of a railroad spur connecting Abilene to Santa Fe would soon become a reality. He would own a good portion of the land in southeastern Colorado, land that the rumors guessed the railroad would cut through, and which would be worth a gold mine. When the time was right, he planned to be on the receiving end of a bucketload of money.

There was only one reason he could fail. And he had no intention of allowing anyone to stand between himself and the fortune he planned to make.

He had to find a way to stop her.

Sykes was not due to arrive for another few days. Then at least he'll have taken care of Ryan, his biggest problem. That man was harder to get rid of than fleas on a hound dog. Sykes had a reputation with a six-gun. Anyone Sykes shot, he killed. Emerson was fully prepared to pay out as much as five hundred dollars to get the job done.

Moving the telegram to the upper left-hand corner of his desk, he picked up a copy of the stagecoach schedule and the *Milford Gazette*. Though the newspaper was not a big one, it contained the information he needed. More than one leg of the stage had been attacked in recent weeks, either by outlaws or Indians. He'd have to send for Foster—he could be counted on to do whatever he was asked, quickly and cleanly. He'd not been caught yet; only Boyle had. The only reason he hadn't used Foster to go after Ryan was the need to make it appear as if a lone gunman killed the wealthy ranchowner. Foster would be able to get rid of the female.

Leaning back against the leather-cushioned chair, he laced his fingers together and rested them on his stomach. He tried to imagine what Ryan's sister would look like. Drawing a blank, he finally decided to go on the assumption that she looked like her brother. She'd be rawboned like Ryan, possibly five and a half feet tall, with wavy ink-black hair. Heaven help the woman if she shared the same craggy features. Ryan's horse looked a darn sight better than Ryan did.

Jotting down the brief description, he folded the bit of paper into a small square, slipped it into his vest pocket, and patted it for good measure.

"Sheridan!"

His young assistant poked his head through the door and waited for his summons before entering.

Emerson motioned for him to come in, then pointed toward the telegram on the corner of his desk. "See to it that that gets delivered to Ryan today."

His assistant looked down at the wire, then back up at him and opened his mouth to speak.

"Now," Emerson bit out. He had no intention of explaining how Ryan's telegram had come to be in his possession. Sheridan was fairly new. He would learn not to question him.

"Right away, sir."

He watched the young man sweep the piece of paper off the desk and start to dash out of the room, as if the lad's heels were on fire, when he remembered something else.

"Sheridan!"

The young man stopped, one hand on the edge of the open door. "Sir?"

"Send word to Foster that I want to see him tonight at the house."

"Yes, sir."

Maggie smiled at the slender dark-haired woman climbing into the stage, settling on the seat opposite of her.

"Good mornin' to ye," she said pleasantly.

"It will be, when this last leg of the journey is behind me," the woman grumbled.

"Me name's Maggie. I'm goin' as far as Emerson."

The driver cracked his whip and set the team of horses in motion.

"Sarah Worthington," her fellow passenger said. Her grumbling was less noticeable now that they were actually on their way out of town.

"I won't be stopping in Emerson," the woman said.

Maggie had hoped the woman's bleak mood would improve with the journey. Sometimes the close confines of the stage encouraged conversation. She sighed, glancing over at the still-silent Sarah, and was struck by the sudden thought that Sarah reminded her of Seamus. She was tall and thin, like her brother. *Unlike those of us who are short, with flesh to spare,* she thought to herself. With Sarah's luxurious dark hair and cool blue eyes, she could be mistaken for Seamus's sister . . . more so than she ever would.

"Sarah," she began, "have ye any relatives in Ireland?"

Sarah smiled and shook her head. "My mother's people are from Wales."

"That's grand," Maggie said excitedly. "I've a cousin on me mother's side that's from—"

The crack of a rifle shot cut off the rest of her words. The coach lurched, then gradually stopped. Not again!

"Are we being held up?" Sarah asked, worry creasing a line between her raven brows.

"Have ye a weapon?"

The other woman shook her head.

"Whatever ye do, don't scream," Maggie suggested. "It rattles the driver and scares the horses."

"I promise—"

The barrel of a six-gun appeared in the open window.

Before either woman could think to act, the gun went off and Sarah slumped over in her seat, crimson staining the right side of her pale-blue cotton dress.

Maggie waited until the gun disappeared from the window, then threw herself across to the other seat.

"Joshua . . . what would ye do, if ye were here?" she wondered aloud, as she tore a strip off the bottom edge of one of her petticoats. Folding it quickly, she thought of the extra cloth Annie had packed in her carpetbag. How wise Annie had been. If she intended to live out here, she would have to start carrying around supplies for just this sort of occasion. Until then, she'd just have to make do and hope Sarah's wound would stop bleeding soon.

Her own rescuer had been calm, she remembered, the only sign of emotion showing in his tightly clenched jaw and beautiful green eyes.

"At least I don't have to remove an arrow—" Maggie paused, then gasped, "The bullet!"

The sound of a horse riding away didn't deter Maggie from the need to search for an exit wound. Though Sarah was larger than she, Maggie was able to brace the woman against her chest as she searched Sarah's back. The sight of a slowly spreading bloodstain on Sarah's back brought with it a sigh of relief that the bullet had gone clean through, but also the worry that she had two wounds to care for.

Working quickly, she ripped off another strip and fashioned another square and a bandage that she could wrap around Sarah. Sticking her head out of the window, she was surprised to see dust in the distance. A wagon was heading toward them.

"Hello!" a sultry voice called out. "Anyone hurt?"

"Luann?!" Maggie opened the door and leapt down

from the coach, totally unaware that the bodice of her dress was smeared with Sarah's blood.

"You're bleeding!"

Maggie looked down at herself and saw the stains for the first time. "Not mine—Sarah's—she needs help."

"What about the driver?" Luann asked, nodding toward the top of the stage. The driver was slumped over, his big body tangled in the reins. No wonder they had slowed down, Maggie thought.

"I'll check. We need to get Sarah someplace safe." Halfway up the side of the coach, she stopped. "I think I may know why we were attacked," she said slowly. Luann waited, but Maggie shook her head. "Later."

Hauling herself up on the top, she swallowed the fear edging up her throat and touched the man. He groaned. "He's alive!" she shouted down.

"See if you can rouse him, while I get Sarah into my carriage."

"He needs a doctor." Maggie gritted her teeth, sat the driver upright, then gently shook him. "Can ye hear me?"

"I'm not deaf," the man grumbled.

"Well now, I'm certain to be thankful for small favors," she bit out.

The driver opened one eye and had the audacity to glare at her. Maggie decided then and there that he'd survive. He looked too stubborn to let a little thing like a bullet keep him down.

"Can ye help me?"

"You been shot too?"

She shook her head no.

"Well then, what do you need my help for?" he demanded. "I ain't gonna be much help—been shot, ya know."

Maggie swallowed the sharp retort poised on the tip

of her tongue and looked up at the deep blue sky, searching the endless blue for a way to rein in her impatience.

"I can't lift ye," she explained. "Can ye move?"

It took a few minutes before he understood her. When he did, he actually smiled. "Why didn't ya say so."

Maggie tore off another strip of her petticoat and wrapped it around the wound in the driver's thigh. But it still bled.

"You'll have to tie another one around my leg above the wound," he told her. "Tie it tight enough, and it'll stop the bleeding."

Maggie did as she was bid.

"Real tight," he reminded her.

When he was satisfied, he let her help him down.

"How far are we from your place, Luann?"

"Half a mile."

"Sarah needs help."

"Doc Simpson's seeing to Betty Lou and her new baby," Luann said.

Maggie knew Luann was watching closely for a reaction. After all Ida had told her about the woman, she thought she knew what Luann waited for. It just wouldn't be the response Luann expected. Maggie smiled at her. "Then let's go."

The driver limped over to check his team and then nodded in the direction Luann had mentioned. "I'll follow along behind; no sense leaving my team at the mercy of outlaws."

"Do ye feel well enough?" Maggie watched the way the man swayed as he walked back to the coach. He nodded and put his leg up to prepare to climb back on top, but his wounded leg folded up underneath him.

As she braced an arm around him, she asked, "Can ye lead the way?"

The other woman smiled, realizing what Maggie was suggesting. "You'll be sure to follow right behind?"

"Aye. If I can convince Mr.—"

"Seth," he grumbled, limping to the door Maggie held open for him.

"I'll drive Mr. Seth and his team."

"Just Seth," he grumbled. "Dad-blamed female," he complained, hoisting himself inside the coach. "Get a-going," he ordered.

Maggie climbed up into the driver's seat. She grabbed the reins and released the brake, clicking her tongue the way she had for her father's horse on those few occasions when she had been allowed to drive their wagon into town.

"Joshua," she whispered, "I need yer help. Me brother's in trouble. And I think someone just tried to kill me."

"Sheriff!" Joshua called out, pounding on the jailhouse door.

Though the hour was still early, he'd seen a light burning in the back window. Either the sheriff had someone locked up, or he had spent the night catching up on some paperwork and had yet to leave.

Sheriff Coltrane opened the door and stood there shaking his head, a single piece of paper clutched in his left hand. Joshua's senses jumped up and started twitching. Something in the man's stance indicated there was a problem. He'd seen that same look before.

Two summers back, Jed Slater had looked up at him from where he sat cradling his injured wife in his arms. Joshua remembered the way his gut clenched, unsure if the woman would survive the beating she'd taken at the hands of the outlaws who had tried to take Slater's ranch. Even the news that the outlaws had been captured had not eased the anguish from Slater's eyes. No longer new to the job of marshal, Joshua agreed with him. Nothing would replace Essie Slater, or ever make up for the fact that she had been attacked. She had taken him in after she had found him wandering the back alleyways of Denver nearly a decade and a half ago and had been a surrogate mother to him. Essie fed him and hugged him when he was too tired and lonely to care what happened to him. His young man's pride never seemed to stop her from doing what she'd seen as her duty, even when she took to hugging him in public.

Over the years since the Slaters had found him, he slowly healed from the devastating loss of his parents enough to dedicate his life to the pursuit of justice. He could never bring his parents back, but he could try to protect the Essie and Jed Slaters of the world. The hardest blow in his later years had been the realization that he could not protect the ones he loved every minute of the day. He already knew bad things happened to good people, but the added knowledge that he could not always be there for those he loved was a bitter pill to swallow.

He muttered under his breath, and set his memories aside. One thing he had learned over the years was to pay attention to the warning signs his instincts gave him. The prickling of unease that crept up his spine, the wave of cold that swept over the back of his neck, or the knots of tension in his gut. Right now, standing there facing the sheriff of Emerson, he felt all three. Whatever the news, it was not good.

At the other lawman's continued silence, he decided to tend to the business at hand.

"We caught these men rustling cattle over at the Ryan spread."

The sheriff's head snapped up, and the look in his eyes

cleared instantly. "Bring 'em in," he said, tossing a ring of keys toward Joshua.

He deftly caught the ring and motioned for the men to be brought inside. Reilly and Flynn shoved the men through the doorway and prodded them to walk down the hallway, using the barrels of their rifles to keep the men walking.

Once the outlaws were untied and the doors to their cell safely locked, the men headed back down the hall to where the sheriff still stood gazing down at a piece of paper in his hand.

"Coltrane?"

The haunted eyes that met his gaze had uneasiness snaking back up his spine.

"Whatever news you've got, can't be good," Joshua said slowly. "No sense keeping it all to yourself. Let's have it."

Reilly and Flynn moved to stand on either side of him, waiting for the sheriff to tell them the news.

"The stage to Emerson was ambushed five miles outside of Milford."

"Any word on who did it?"

"None."

"Anyone injured?"

The sheriff's pale-gray eyes misted over, and he audibly cleared his throat. "The driver and one of the two women passengers."

Joshua felt his gut clench, then ice over. Maggie was due to get back on the stage as soon as she felt well enough. Could it be her? "How badly?"

"The driver was shot. The bullet bounced off his thighbone. . . ."

Impatient for Coltrane to finish, he prodded him to continue. "And the women?"

"One was shot, the other is missing," the sheriff said, laying the paper on his desk.

All of the air left Joshua's lungs, and his vision grayed. "Have either been identified?"

It cost him to speak the words without any inflection, to appear outwardly in control. Inside, his mind screamed at the injustice of living in a territory so new to statehood, large sections of it were still patrolled by the Army. The lawless preyed on the innocent without mercy. His heart bled, tormented by the image of his Maggie lying unconscious and bleeding.

"The information is scarce yet. I'm waiting for another wire with descriptions of both women." Coltrane turned and reached for four mugs and snatched the steaming coffeepot off the pot-bellied stove in the corner of the room.

Joshua noticed the man's hands shaking, as he poured the thick black brew, sloshing it over the brim of one cup. He waited for the older man to get himself back under control. There must be more to the story than he was telling, Joshua thought. Anyone who spent his life chasing outlaws and trying to right wrongs usually ended up either sacrificing the love of a good woman in order to uphold the law, or losing someone dear to him because of that same job.

Before either of them could lift a cup to sip the strong brew, the door to the jail burst open and James Ryan stormed inside, a crumpled bit of paper clutched in his fist.

"I just heard about the stage!" he said, his chest heaving.

Joshua noticed Ryan had the look of a man on the verge of violence. "Did you know one of the passengers?"

"Aye, my . . . Maggie."

Joshua heard the words, and wondered how many Maggies could be traveling by stage to the town of Emerson. The tortured look in Ryan's eyes, and the anguish in his raspy voice as he spoke Maggie's name, arrowed through Joshua. Whoever this Maggie was, it was obvious to everyone in the room that Ryan loved her.

"Can you write a description?" the sheriff asked. "I can send a wire over to the sheriff in Milford."

Ryan took the pen the sheriff offered, dipped it in the inkwell, and tried to put the words to paper, but his hand shook so badly, the ink blotted across the paper.

"Here," Reilly said, "let me."

"But ye don't know what she looks like," Ryan protested.

"I've heard ye wax poetic on how she looks for the last five years," Reilly shot back.

Joshua noticed a similar look of anguished worry on both Reilly and Flynn's faces. This woman meant a great deal to all of them.

"Start with her height, then hair color, and eyes," the sheriff advised.

"She's a just a wee bit of woman, comes up to here on me," Ryan said slowly, holding the flat of his hand even with the bottom edge of his breastbone.

"A little over five feet high," Joshua said through gritted teeth . . . the same height as the Maggie he knew. The sheriff nodded, agreeing with his estimation of the height.

"Hair as red as Flynn's with eyes blue as himself," Reilly added, pointing toward Ryan.

Could it be the same woman? Fate would not be so cruel, would it? He'd only just found her. They had sealed their vows in blood, just like his Scottish ancestors. . . . Well, not exactly the same way, but their blood had mingled and their souls had connected. She was his! In his dreams, Maggie would be waiting for him.

"Ye've never seen her!" Flynn bit out.

"Aye, but Jamie here's told us so often, Flynn's taken to wearin' his hat indoors, just to keep Jamie from remarkin' his hair being just like Maggie's," Reilly added.

Joshua looked over at Ryan and saw a ghost of a smile start to form, then swiftly disappear. He knew how Ryan felt. He'd been tempted to sink his fingers in Maggie's hair, compelled to touch the fire in it, wondering if it would be hot to the touch. Would he be burned?

"She has such lovely skin . . . roses and cream, with freckles across her nose," Ryan choked out.

Joshua was nearly undone by the man's pain. He'd have to be dead not to see the love Ryan felt for Maggie. Though his breath snagged in his chest, and his heart felt as if it were being wrung mercilessly by unseen hands, he struggled to keep his slipping control in place.

She's the one . . . but not mine . . . she belongs to Ryan.

"I'll not be waiting for you to send the wire," Ryan said, his blue eyes blazing with inner fire. "I just stopped by to make sure you've locked up the rustlers before I ride for Milford."

"You're not going alone, Jamie," Reilly said, placing a restraining hand on his arm.

"We'll ride with ye," Flynn added.

"Who will run your ranch?" Joshua asked, hoping to distract Ryan and convince him not to interfere with the law. He needed Ryan to stay behind for two reasons. The first, his desire to see for himself that the injured woman was not the woman he feared. The second, he was planning on finding the missing woman. If it was his Maggie, then he wanted to hear from her own soft lips that Ryan meant nothing to her . . . that he was a

cousin, or a friend of the family—anything but her intended. He could not and would not accept that the
woman who had melted so smoothly into his embrace
could love another.

"Masterson and the Murphys can handle things while
I'm away."

So much for Ryan staying behind. As if he would in
Ryan's place, he thought to himself.

"We're set on coming as well," Reilly added.

Ryan nodded that he'd heard, before turning on his
heel and heading out the door.

Joshua started to follow the other men, when the sheriff called him back. "After I send this wire, I'll be expecting a description of the women. If you can convince
Ryan to wait for just a bit, it might save us a heap of
trouble down the road."

Joshua started to disagree, then thought of something
he could use. "Why don't you go on after Ryan and tell
him you need him to sign some papers to keep the rustlers behind bars. While you do that, I'll head on over
to the telegraph office, send in my report on the rustlers,
and wait for the women's descriptions from the sheriff
in Milford."

Coltrane nodded and went after Ryan.

Alone, but for the muted conversations echoing down
the hallway from the jail cells, Joshua hung his head and
sent out a silent prayer that Ryan's Maggie was the missing woman. *Just please don't let her be the same woman
I cradled in my arms.*

He couldn't bear it if Ryan would be the one to dip
his head down and inhale the haunting scent of lavender
and rain.

Reason slowly filtered through his aching head as he
walked toward the telegraph office. He'd been unable to
fight the attraction from the first. Though he felt the con-

nection they shared was soul-deep and binding, Maggie might feel differently. In fact, he had no idea how she felt about him. Other than the trust he'd seen in her eyes when he was taking care of her wound, he was unsure of just what she thought of him. He'd not pressed her the last time he'd seen her, he thought grimly. He had all but ignored the need to enfold her in his arms and hold her against his chest. He had needed to focus on the job at hand and could not afford to let himself be distracted. He had tamped down the need to find her, gather her in his arms, and lean the side of his face in her hair and breathe in her scent. He had been a gentleman. Being gentlemanly may have just cost him the love of his life.

With that cold thought running through his body like ice, he strode into the small office and nodded to the man busily copying down a wire transmission. The man glanced over at him, but didn't stop writing. While he watched, the man answered the transmission with a few clicks of his own.

Whether or not either of the women involved in the attack was his Maggie, it was time to find out just where he stood in Maggie Flaherty's eyes.

Chapter Ten

"**D**on't let the doc see you, if you don't want anyone to know you are here," Luann advised.

Maggie smiled and shook her head. "You're a wonder, thinkin' up a way to keep anyone from knowin' where I am. This is the second time ye've come to me aid." She took the other woman's hand in her own. "I cannot thank ye enough."

"Is there anyone you want to send word to, so that someone knows where you are?"

"Can ye send word to the Smiths, tellin' them I'm all right for now?"

"Done."

Maggie could hear the commotion coming from the lower level. She recognized the voice sending a stream of swear words floating up to her. She smiled. The stage-coach driver really hated being cared for by females. And if her guess was right, more than one had flocked

112

downstairs to see to the driver and the barely conscious Sarah. She tried to put the most recent scene from her mind, but the echoing shots and terrifying sight of Sarah's blood-spattered gown made it impossible to focus on anything else.

Needing something to do, she pulled a sheet of writing paper out of the dainty painted desk in the corner of the room and began to transcribe one of her grandmother's recipes for mutton stew from memory. While she wrote, another of her mother's recipes came to mind. She scribbled that one down too. A short time later, she had complied quite a few of her brother's well-loved recipes. She intended to surprise him and give his cook a break, by offering her own services temporarily.

But thoughts of both attacks had her wondering if she would live to see her brother again . . . or a certain lawman.

Try to envision yer guardian angel then, mo croi, her mother had often advised, when she'd had bad dreams as a child. Maggie closed her eyes, willing to give it a try now. She focused on the image she'd so often used as a child . . . but the dark-haired warrior angel wielding the immense sword she often pictured, now melded into the image of a green-eyed, golden-haired lawman with broad shoulders, strong hands, and a six-gun.

"I'm not sure where to go or what to do," she said softly to the image of the man she'd come to depend upon in her dreams. "Whom should I trust?" she asked the phantom vision.

"No one," a deep voice called out from the doorway.

She gasped and turned toward the sound of the voice.

"Taylor!" she exclaimed. "What are ye doin' here? Does Ida know ye've come?"

"It was her idea. Once she knew you were safe and unharmed, she sent me off to tell you the latest news."

"What would that be?" She closed the door behind him.

"Sheriff Coltrane, from over in Emerson, has a posse riding this way. They left after they received the wire about the attack."

"Do you know who is riding with him?" Her heart pounded within her breast, as thoughts of Marshal Turner flitted through her tired brain.

"No . . . seems some men from the Ryan place are riding with him, three I think."

"Mr. Ryan himself?" she asked.

Taylor shook his head. "I don't know. Why?"

"I was hopin' to send word to me brother, that I'll be traveling at daybreak."

"Just how do you plan to get there?" Taylor demanded, his back ramrod straight, his eyes blazing at her.

"Ye remind me of my Da," she said softly, laying a hand on his arm. "Ye know I've got to go—the time left is runnin' out."

Taylor looked away, cleared his throat, and looked back at her. "I'll wait until Doc leaves to take the patients with him to his surgery, then we can ride back to town without being seen."

When she would have protested, he shook his head. "You are staying with us tonight—no arguments."

She started to speak, but his determined look stopped her. She nodded her agreement.

"I'll go down to the kitchen and rustle up some coffee and something to eat. Stay put."

She smiled. He had a hand on the doorknob, but paused before opening the door.

"I'll be riding with you at daybreak," he said over his shoulder. "I'll have two horses saddled and ready to go."

"How can I thank ye and Ida for all ye've done for me?"

"By not getting into any more trouble."

Maggie walked toward him grinning and hugged him tightly. "Ye know, I've tried more than once, but I can't seem to help meself. Trouble comes lookin' for me—I don't go lookin' for it."

She heard Taylor's low sigh and watched as he made his way down the back staircase into the kitchen.

"You look dead on your feet, Maggie," Ida observed hours later.

Nearly cross-eyed with fatigue, Maggie did not wonder whether or not Ida was right. She was more concerned with walking down the long hallway to her room without having to ask for help. She hated to admit to being tired or weak. She had a two-day journey ahead of her at daybreak. Getting as much rest as she could was at the top of her list of things to do right now.

"I think I'll turn in," she said, touching the white linen napkin to her lips before folding it neatly and setting it next to her dinner plate.

"Do you need my help?" Ida asked.

"Not just yet," she replied, not wanting to intrude upon Ida's time with her husband. The thought that she'd be taking him away from Ida for the next few days bothered her. But it was the only way they would let her go. "Enjoy the rest of your meal. No need to rush."

Maggie made her way down the narrow passageway in a daze, struggling to keep her eyelids from closing before she made it to the door to her room. She intended to sit for a while and read through some of her sheet music. But since there was no piano nearby, maybe she'd opt to read through some of the recipes she had copied earlier that afternoon. It had been too long since she'd had the opportunity to bake. Her fingers itched to sink into a bowl of bread dough or fashion a fluted crust for a pie.

"I'll be glad to see Seamus and the grand kitchen he's been writing about," she murmured with a sigh.

The five years since she had last seen him stretched before her like the endless miles of ocean they had crossed together. Soon . . . she'd hold her brother in her arms and feel his strength surround her. Their parting hug had nearly crushed her ribs and broken her heart, but her brother's hopes and dreams were worth every tear she shed missing him. She could wait a few more days.

Maggie laid a hand against the door and pushed it open the rest of the way.

"Me mind must be playin' tricks . . . I though I'd left it closed altogether."

The bedclothes hung half on the bed, half off. The dresser drawers had been upended; her unmentionables heaped in the middle of the floor. Walking toward the pile, she recognized the tiny bits of white as the remains of her precious sheet music.

"My things—"

Her breath snagged in her throat at the sound of a floorboard creaking just behind her. She whirled back toward the sound, and the sight that met her disbelieving eyes nearly caused her heart to stop beating.

A tall, wiry man stood between her and the door. Dressed in black from hat to boots, he blended in with the shadows. Heaven help her, she must have walked right past him. The bottom half of his face was hidden by a dusty, stained bandanna, leaving only his small dark eyes and slashing black brows accenting the top half of his crooked nose.

One look at the cold hard gaze he leveled at her, and she felt the bottom drop out of her stomach. Her legs went numb with terror unlike anything she had ever experienced before. The frozen feeling crept up past her knees, all the way to her chest.

Maggie wet her lips with her tongue and tried to clear her throat, but could not budge the lump of overwhelming fear lodged there. By the time her mind processed the man's menacing stance and urged her to run, he had closed the distance between them. Before the scream bottled up in her frozen chest could burst free, he clapped an immense gloved hand across her open mouth, and spun her around until her back was plastered to his front.

A cold sweat broke out behind her knees.

With a deftness and strength beyond her comprehension, he slipped a gag over her mouth, yanked her arms behind her, and tied them.

Her breath came in short gasps. She could not get enough air. With a will of iron, she closed her eyes and tried to focus on something . . . anything . . . to calm her breathing. Her frantic thoughts skipped back and forth until finally she knew what to think about . . . the last time she felt safe. Immediately, the welcome image of broad shoulders and brilliant green eyes filled her. But the rag tasted foul, of sweat and dirt. She started to gag—she needed air!

The room swayed, her knees buckled, and her world went black.

"Maggie?"

Ida knocked a bit louder and put her ear to the door, but didn't hear a sound.

"Poor mite's exhausted," she said, quietly opening the door.

Standing in the middle of the small room, Ida felt her head begin to swim. The reason for the chaos that greeted her didn't register at first. But as the seconds ticked past, a feeling of dread settled deep in her bones, chilling her.

Maggie was gone. From the looks of what was left of her things, she had been taken by force.

"Taylor!" Ida screamed for all she was worth.

The sound of her husband's boot heels swiftly pounding on the hardwood floor as he raced to her side, were of little comfort to her. Maggie was gone—someone had kidnapped her.

The familiar sight of her husband's bespectacled face as he burst through the open doorway went a long way toward soothing her frayed nerves. He took one look at the shambles, and let out a low whistle.

"What happened?" he asked, running a hand through his closely cropped iron-gray hair.

"Someone kidnapped Maggie."

He wrapped an arm around her, and Ida felt herself being propelled through the door down the hallway to the kitchen.

"Drink this."

A short squat glass was thrust into her hand. She stared down at the amber-colored liquid . . . and for an awful moment, she imagined the worst. Maggie was gone and they would never find her. The poor young woman had placed her trust in them, and they had failed her.

Strong hands clasped her upper arms.

"Snap out of it, Ida." She heard the strain in her husband's voice and hung on to the sound of it like a lifeline, depending upon him to pull her out of the swirling darkness that threatened.

The cool smooth edge of the glass touched her lips a heartbeat before the potent whiskey burned a fiery trail down her throat. She coughed.

Through watery eyes, she looked up at the concern-lined face inches from her own. "We have to find her."

"Will you be all right while I go fetch the sheriff?"

She nodded her head.

"I'll be back before you miss me," he said, pressing a swift kiss to her forehead.

Ida raised a hand to touch the side of his face, but he was already gone. With a supreme effort, she began to pull herself together, telling herself it wouldn't do Maggie any good to fall to pieces. Lifting the glass to her lips, she downed the contents in one gulp.

Her eyes crossed and her chest burned, but she felt a bit steadier.

Fifteen minutes later, when Sheriff Roscoe and her husband came in through the back door, she was ready to do her part to help track down Maggie's kidnappers.

Chapter Eleven

Sharp pain sliced through the left side of Maggie's head as it bounced against the horse's flank, keeping time with the fast trot. Closing her eyes kept the dirt and grit the horse's front hooves kicked up out of them, but there was nothing she could do about her roiling stomach.

Maggie mumbled a heartfelt prayer under her breath that someone would find them before all the life was bounced out of her. She had no idea how long she'd been lying facedown across the stranger's packhorse, but it was better than the way she'd started the trip, flung across his lap, with the edge of her jaw pounding against the side of his knee. She flexed her jaw and winced. A bone-deep ache radiated from below her ear all the way to her chin.

She refused to be embarrassed just because she'd started to retch on the dreadful man's boots. He'd been quiet up until she'd started gagging. Her tender ears stilled burned from the litany of curses he'd flung at her, though it was surely a sign of providence that he stopped long enough to lift her off his lap and deposit her on the packhorse. Although if she had a choice, she would be sitting.

One thought kept worrying her—the two bedrolls, and after a quick glance, what appeared to be cookware and supplies. Was one of those bedrolls for her? If it was, just how many days did he intend to keep her hostage? The supplies the silent man carried would last more than a week. Fear coiled tightly within her breast, making it even harder to draw in a deep breath.

Crossing the dark foaming Atlantic Ocean had not scared the breath out of her, but the prospect of being alone with this stranger for more than one day was simply terrifying. Just being next to the man made her flesh creep and her heart pound.

Please let him stop soon.

As if she had spoken the words aloud, the horse obeyed and came to an abrupt halt. Maggie strained to listen, hoping to hear anything that sounded familiar. Though what would sound familiar way out here in the middle of nowhere, she had no idea. She focused on her surroundings, ignoring the pounding in her head and the rush of blood through her veins. Then she heard it—the soothing sound of water tumbling over rocks was music to her ears. If the man had stopped to water the horses, maybe she would have a chance to wash the awful taste from her mouth. Maybe she could convince the man to keep from gagging her. While she was at it, she'd ask to ride astride instead of upside-down like a sack of potatoes.

The saddle creaked; the sound of spurs jingling told her he had dismounted. The quiet that followed was unnerving. Where was he now? She turned her head to better hear the sound of hooves, boots, or breathing—anything that would tell her she had not been abandoned in the middle of the night. In the middle of nowhere!

Just when she thought she couldn't stand the wait, she was roughly hauled from the horse and set on her feet. The action was so swift, the blood that had pooled in her brain from hanging upside-down rushed all the way down to her toes. Her legs promptly folded up beneath her, and she felt herself sliding toward the ground.

The air was suddenly ripe with cursing, as the man placed his hands beneath her arms and lifted her up until she was eye level. Cold dark eyes glared at her. Stark fear blended with panic, and for a moment, her brain ceased to function.

She could not move. Maggie did not see a spark of life in those eyes. They were the eyes of a killer. Her tongue felt paralyzed. There was no point in trying to speak.

A heartbeat later, her brain kicked in and along with it the words of warning she had often heard growing up. *The devil and his minions walk the earth.*

Dizzy from the unorthodox ride through the country, and the possibility she was about to meet her doom, Maggie was tempted to give in to the darkness swirling about her. It would be a blessing after all she'd been through in the last few hours.

"Never give up!"

Da? Maggie shook her head to clear it, focusing on the face in front of her. Slashing black brows and hard dark eyes left little hope of softness from the man, but she knew in her heart that she couldn't give up hope. Her Da would never have encouraged her to give in.

A flicker in the depths of his dark gaze changed the

intense expression. "Promise not to scream, and I'll remove the gag."

She nodded so hard, the remaining pins came loose and her hair slipped free from the topknot Ida had helped her fashion.

The man's eyes widened and an expression she began to dread crossed his hard features. She bit back the need to scream and instead offered up another silent prayer. Maggie held her breath when he reached around the back of her head, then let it go in a whoosh of air as the gag slipped free.

"Thank you," she said, working her jaw, ignoring the pain on the left side of it. It would be an ugly bruise, she knew.

He nodded, then turned to walk the horses over to the stream. Maggie sighed watching him, wondering if all men were dense, or only the ones with devious intentions. She couldn't follow him without falling flat on her face; her hands were still tightly bound behind her.

"Can ye not untie me hands?" she called out to the retreating man.

He stopped long enough to shake his head no. Maggie couldn't believe the man would let her stand there trussed up like a chicken about to be roasted. "I've a powerful thirst—"

"So do the horses."

Either the man was deliberately pretending to ignore her needs, she thought, or he didn't much care. Probably the latter. Now that she was still, she realized that all that bouncing had affected her in a more urgent way. She had to relieve herself . . . soon.

"I need a few minutes of privacy."

The man was making his way back toward her, the reins to both horses in his right hand. He stopped, spat out a curse, and rubbed a hand across his face. She wondered why he dropped the reins, but the horses were obviously used to it. They walked a short distance away before starting to graze. She had not spent that much time with the pair of plow horses her family kept back in Ireland. Maggie wondered if they would bolt, but after watching them chewing contentedly, she decided they would not try to break free.

Her captor pulled a deadly-looking knife from his belt and held it an inch from her nose. "If you're not back in five minutes, I may be tempted to use this on you," he said, waving the blade back and forth for emphasis.

She nodded her understanding. Though it took a great deal of courage, Maggie turned her back to him so he could slice through the bonds that held her. Hoping he could see well enough in the dark to slice the rope and not her hands, she stood still as a stone.

He grabbed her right hand. The ropes cut into her wrists when he pulled them taut enough to slice through them. With a jerk and a few sawing movements, she was free.

Maggie almost stumbled in her desire to put some distance between herself and the devil's own. She was tempted to rub the stinging sensation from her wrists, but from the way they throbbed, she was afraid she would end up doing more damage. She slipped behind a trio of bushes to answer nature's call, hurrying lest her kidnapper come looking for her with his knife.

"Thank you," she said quietly, once she had rejoined him.

He lifted her into the saddle and let his gaze sweep from the top of her head down to where the tips of her high-buttoned shoes peeked out from beneath her dusty gown. This time she was aware enough to recognize the look in his eyes, and for the first time wondered if she had more to fear from this man than abduction.

Never letting his gaze leave hers, he closed the distance between them until they stood toe to toe. Though it cost her, she tilted her head back, meeting his lust-filled look with one that promised retribution.

When he continued to stare at her, she blurted out, "If ye harm one hair on me head, me brother Seamus'll pound ye into the dirt." Maggie nearly swooned from holding her breath while waiting for him to answer her challenge.

He ran the tip of his gloved forefinger across her cheek. "It'll keep till we reach the cabin."

She sensed she had been granted a reprieve, but for how long?

"Are you satisfied that they've told you all they know?" Ryan asked.

Joshua nodded his agreement. He was positive either the driver or the woman was lying about the attack. Their stories were too pat and sounded rehearsed. They were hiding something. But what? Had they come to after being shot only to find Maggie already gone, or had they watched her slip away? Were they trying to protect her? His head hurt from trying to puzzle it out. He needed coffee.

The one bit of information he and Ryan agreed on was that Maggie Flaherty had been on board that stage. The arrow to his heart bled, the wound grievous, as he realized that Ryan's Maggie was indeed *his* Maggie.

Pacing in front of the sheriff's desk, Joshua tried to piece together what he would say when he found her. Right now the thing they needed to do was find her, quickly, before anything else happened to her.

"Sheriff!" a young sandy-haired man shouted, barreling through the open door. "Mr. Smith said I was to tell you about the rustlers."

"What rustlers?" the sheriff asked, slowly coming to his feet.

"Over by the Ryan place near Emerson," the young man answered.

The foul curse Ryan issued split the air, echoed by Reilly and Flynn.

"You've got to get back to your ranch," Joshua said, setting his hat back on his head.

"I'm going after Maggie."

"I can go after her," Joshua countered. "Besides, I'm better at tracking."

For a moment, he thought Ryan would refuse; the man's face was mottled red with suppressed anger. Joshua had a good idea what Ryan was thinking. He felt a similar rage begin to bubble up within him the moment he'd heard about the attack on the stage coach. Right now it was taking a considerable amount of effort on his part to keep that rage contained.

He watched Ryan run a hand through his hair, then heard the man sigh. "All right, then."

"I'll find her," Joshua promised.

"Your life depends on it," Ryan answered.

Watching Ryan and his men leave, Joshua didn't know if he would have the courage or faith to let another find the woman he loved, while he headed home to fight a battle against rustlers.

"Marshal."

Joshua turned at the sound of yet another man's voice. He recognized Taylor Smith immediately. "What brings you over here? We're just about ready to go."

"I need to speak with you," Smith said, staring around at the other men still gathered in the small jail. "Alone."

Joshua nodded, walked outside, and waited for the older man to follow on behind him.

"I need to get on the trail before it grows cold."

"You need to understand what has been going on with Maggie."

Ice sluiced over into his knotted stomach, fear for the woman he cared for nearly blinding him. This was the exact reason he never let himself get too close to any one of the women who pursued him over the years. He could not afford to let anything happen to the woman he let himself love. He nearly laughed at the idea of letting himself fall in love with Maggie. He'd had no control over his heart from the moment he laid eyes on her. Joshua cleared his throat and swallowed his growing fear. "Tell me."

"Maggie has some very important papers with her," Taylor began. "Papers she must deliver to her brother by Wednesday."

"Seamus?"

"Right, her brother over in Emerson."

"Why is she sending wires to James Ryan?"

Taylor shook his head. "I don't know."

Joshua did—she and Ryan were obviously a couple. He set that thought aside and tried to focus on the rest of what Taylor was telling him.

"—thought when the stage was attacked that she was the target."

"What?" He only caught the second half of what Taylor had said.

"Maggie was worried about the papers she was to carry to her brother. We had the sheriff witness a document stating that the papers did exist, and that we had seen them. When she disappeared off the stage, we were worried it had something to do with those papers."

"What exactly is it that she's carrying?"

"A copy of the deed to her brother's ranch and the paid mortgage. Apparently he's having trouble with the local bank."

"I'm not surprised," Joshua said quietly. "Seems Ryan is having a similar problem. I'll have to make it a point to call on Mr. Emerson and check out his bank."

"Anything else?"

"Yes. She sent word to me from Pearl's place. She was hiding there. Only two people even knew she was there. Luann and myself."

"Why was Maggie here if she was safe hiding at Pearl's?"

"I persuaded her to come back here with me," Taylor said, shaking his head. "I thought I could keep her safe until we left for Emerson at dawn."

"What happened?"

"Did you speak to Luann?"

"Yes. And I believe that she's telling the truth. She doesn't know who kidnapped Maggie. We both agree it all comes back around to her brother and his papers. Are they gone?"

"Didn't Sheriff Roscoe fill you in?"

Joshua nodded. "I just wanted to make sure there wasn't anything else I needed to know before I set out to find her." He paused in front of the doorway to the jail. "I *will* find her."

The look of relief on the older man's face was one he hoped to see on Maggie's face when he did find her. If only he knew what he was going to say to her when he did.

Joshua cleared his mind of all thoughts save one, finding the kidnapper's trail. Tracking was his specialty; he'd never had any difficulty locating a trail before.

You've never had a stake in the outcome before.

The fact that he was coming to care deeply for a woman who might be promised to another disturbed his thought process to the degree that it continued to get in the way of his investigation. He'd been involved in a romance or two over the years he spent enforcing the law as marshal. But the women never got tangled up in his thoughts, never got in the way of his work. It had been easy to separate the two.

But with Maggie, it had been different from the start. They were meant to be together . . . linked. He admired her courage, and enjoyed her sense of humor to the point where he found himself imagining what it would be like to come home after a few weeks on the trail and have her waiting for him.

But it wasn't her personality that had him waking up in the middle of the night. Thoughts of her porcelain-smooth, milk-white skin dominated his dreams the last few nights. Her fiery-red hair should have been warning enough. Although he hadn't actually witnessed it yet, she was bound to have a temper to match that red head. For some unfathomable reason, he wanted to see her temper flare. He had a feeling it would be worth the price of making her mad, just to see the show. His hands positively itched to lose themselves in her glorious hair, and trace the sprinkling of freckles across the bridge of her nose. . . .

"You find what you're looking for down there, Marshal?"

Joshua's stomach clenched, and an icy coldness settled deep in the pit of it. In the last few hours that they'd been trying to locate the kidnapper's trail out of town, he'd lost his focus more than once and been thinking of Maggie.

It had to stop. Now.

Concentrating on the two sets of prints, the analytical side of his brain finally kicked in. "These are the same prints."

"But the others over there—" Sheriff Coltrane began.

"—don't quite match the set we found near the Smiths' store." Joshua motioned for the sheriff to come and look more closely at the hoofprints.

"You see right here"—he pointed at the oddly shaped print—"this horse is about to throw a shoe."

He brushed the dirt off his hands, placed a hand on his knee, and rose to his feet. "Let's go."

The miles added up, though it was slow going trying not to disturb the tracks. An hour later, the trail abruptly changed. Joshua got down off his horse and knelt beside the churned-up earth.

"Signs of a struggle." He scanned the ground, walked a few paces to the left, then back to the right. The implications of just what type of struggle occurred broke through the barrier he had erected to keep his mind focused and his worry in its place.

Logically. Think logically.

The others in the search party pulled up and dismounted, but kept a careful distance from the prints. Joshua studied the pattern until his eyes crossed, then finally something caught his eye. He moved over to where the two sets of prints continued and touched his fingers to the packed dirt inside the one horseshoe-shaped mark, and then the other with the loose shoe. Going back over to the prints before the scuffle, he touched the packed dirt inside both sets of prints. Just as he suspected, the depth was different.

"What do you see, Marshal?" one of the men asked.

"They were riding double up to this point." He indicated with the sweep of his arm toward the churned-up earth. "See, here," he said as the group converged around him, "the depth of the prints is more even."

"Do you think he got rid of her?" another in the group asked quietly.

Joshua shook his head. "No. Whatever his reasons for

taking Miss Flaherty, I'm betting they must have been important enough to break into the Smiths' home while it was still early. He risked being seen."

Sheriff Coltrane nodded his agreement. "Whoever it is, whatever his reason, I don't think he'd bring her all the way out here just to get rid of her. Best to fan out. Check the undergrowth, the bushes . . . look for clues . . . anything. A hank of red hair, a bit of white petticoat."

Joshua admired the line of reasoning that was obviously going on behind the sheriff's shrewd gray eyes. He nodded his agreement.

Half a dozen pairs of eyes looked from the sheriff to himself and back. One by one the men mounted up and moved out.

Hanging on to the saddle horn, he put his boot in the stirrup, swung his leg over, and settled in the saddle. Careful to keep an eye and part of his concentration on the trail, he let the rest of it puzzle on the possible reasons for the abduction.

Maggie was a stranger to these parts, wasn't she?

She had no kin. . . . well, none that he had heard of.

The Smiths were good people, honest people. He'd questioned them and quite a few of the townspeople as well. Not one person seemed to have a reason to hold a grudge against them.

Either there was something the Smiths were hiding or there was something Maggie was hiding. Random kidnappings were rare, but the reasons behind the ones he'd investigated had one thing in common—money or revenge.

"How far do you figure they'll travel tonight?" the sheriff asked, interrupting his train of thought.

He grunted, then looked over at the man riding alongside him. "Depends on how much trouble Miss Flaherty gives him." He nearly smiled at the thought. He could imagine her dealing out quite a bit . . . *so long as she's conscious,* his brain reminded him.

"Is there anything that sticks out in your mind about where Miss Flaherty and Mrs. Smith visited recently?" He hoped the sheriff would say something that would give him a clue as to the why of it.

"Can't say that I do . . . unless—"

"What?"

"Well, it didn't seem peculiar at the time, but Ida mentioned Miss Flaherty wanting to send a message out to the Ryan place."

Joshua's hands tightened on the reins, while he unconsciously tensed every muscle in his body. Blaze reacted by throwing his head back and sidestepping. He bent forward and patted the side of the horse's neck, settling him down. "Easy, boy."

He knew all about the wire Ryan received. Being reminded of it brought back the very real problem he would be facing when he confronted Maggie about her feelings for Ryan. He could ask Ryan flat-out what Maggie meant to him, but the man was too distracted. Besides, Joshua was not willing to give up on the vital young woman with eyes the color of cornflowers just yet. If Ryan admitted she was his fiancée, Joshua would have no other option but to step aside. He wasn't ready to give up on the woman he was fast coming to realize held his heart in her hand. He'd decided to hold onto the image of her sharing his life just a bit longer.

"Marshal!" one of the men called out. "I think I've found something."

Chapter Twelve

The cabin her captor spoke about was little more than a falling down lean-to with holes in the roof. The fact that he seemed to be as surprised at the cabin's condition as she made her wonder if someone else was involved in her abduction. Either that, or it had been some time since he had seen the cabin.

The distant rumble of thunder actually eased the growing tension, giving them something else to worry about.

"Do ye think the wind'll blow the storm our way?"

The man looked up at the sky and shook his head. "Hard to tell. The wind could change anytime."

Not a very hopeful response from someone who ought to know the area better than she did, or at least she hoped he did. A blue-white fork of lightning split the sky. The answering rumble of thunder seemed a bit louder than the last.

The wind picked up and whipped a strand of hair into

134

her eyes. They teared in response to the lashing, making it impossible to see.

"I can't see."

"You don't need to."

The gruff reply did little to settle the unease that skittered through her empty stomach. She hoped he didn't plan on forcing his attentions on her, but planned to be ready to defend herself, in case he decided to follow through with his cryptic hints now that they had reached the cabin.

She closed her eyes and willed her rebellious stomach to settle. With every ounce of her being, she forced the man before her to the back of her thoughts and projected another in its place. Behind her closed lids, broad shoulders, large hands, and a crooked smile eased the tension within her.

"Joshua," she whispered.

Thoughts of him had kept her sane while she'd been slung across her kidnapper's lap. Refusing to give in at the first sign of adversity, she kept Joshua's image close to her heart, replaying the first time she'd met him over and over in her mind. Each time, she felt the same awe-inspiring confidence in his ability to calmly remove the arrow and deliver her to safety. As outrageous as it seemed, Maggie hoped he would come to her rescue again. Then she just wished he'd get on with whatever part he would play in her future. She was anxious to begin a new life in Colorado—one she hoped he'd be a part of.

"Time to go inside." The gravel-rough sound of her captor's voice snapped her back to reality.

"Can ye untie me hands . . . please?"

He stood with one hand on the saddle horn and the other on her knee. Though it was full dark and she could not see his features clearly, she could imagine his small dark eyes and leering expression. A feeling of dread snaked up her spine, chilling her to the bone.

From the way he squeezed her knee, he must have thought the shiver of disgust was one of excitement. Maggie was wise enough to hold her tongue, though it plagued her to keep quiet.

Without a word he reached behind her and untied the ropes. Maggie wondered what had happened to the first length of rope he had used to tie her hands. She tried to remember if he had slipped it into his saddlebags, but couldn't. A spark of hope flickered to life within her breast. Maybe someone would find the two small lengths of rope and wonder what could be small enough to be tied with them. Maybe they'd notice that the rope had been cut. Maybe—

Her thoughts were cut off as her muscles awakened with a vengeance. Pins and needles shot through her upper arms and between her shoulder blades. She started to stifle a groan then thought better of it. Maybe it would be to her benefit to appear weak. Before she could decide how to act, she was hauled out of the saddle and set unceremoniously on her feet. Her stiff legs, not used to traveling such distances on horseback, buckled underneath her. She went down like a stone.

Her cheek scraped against something rough and damp, probably a wet tree stump. Vaguely she wondered at the dampness, but before she could form two thoughts, she was lifted off the ground and being carried into the cabin. She was irritated at the way her captor continued to unceremoniously haul her about.

Her captor kicked the door open and strode into the one-room shack. "Not much, but it'll get us out of the storm."

Lightning flashed, illuminating the room long enough for Maggie to notice a fireplace, small table, broken chair, and a pile heaped next to the door. The next flash of light confirmed what she thought she saw: the pile was their supplies.

"Can you stand?"

"I think the feeling's come back to me legs." Deciding to try not to anger her kidnapper, she ignored the way her teeth rattled as he plopped her on her feet. She had more urgent worries. The long night ahead of them, for one. If he had any plan to act on his baser instincts, she would have to be ready and somehow outwit him. She had to come up with a plan to keep him from trying to take advantage of her.

Just then an ear-splitting crack shook the cabin and spooked the horses tied up outside.

"Stay here."

Since she had no intention of disobeying his abrupt command—yet—Maggie waited quietly while he went back outside to see to the horses. A series of flashes and answering rumbles kept her company while he was gone. Maybe she could manage to slip outside while he was busy tending to the horses.

The door to the cabin flung open and rocked back on its hinges. "Glad you didn't try to make a run for it."

Maggie thought quickly and answered, "With a storm ragin' overhead and havin' no idea where we are?" If she acted surprised that he'd give her credit for thinking to escape, she may be able to convince him she was weak-willed. She quickly scratched the first plan of bolting for the door and decided to work with something he would have no trouble believing. Namely that she was a weak and helpless female and escape was the furthest thing from her mind.

The continuous flashing and resounding crashes of thunder indicated the storm was either right overhead or awfully close to it.

"So long as you don't stand out in the open, the storm won't hurt you."

The advice seemed sound, but the need to do just that was quickly becoming the focus of her plan. "Do ye think we can light a fire?" she asked, rubbing her hands up and down her arms, trying to look cold.

He nodded and moved around the dark interior; at the moment the lightning was their only source of light. Her guess that the only source of wood would be the table and chair proved to be correct. The next thing she heard was the splintering of wood. At least the furniture would be of some use, she mused.

Maggie wondered what he'd use to light the fire, but remembered the pile heaped on the floor. He must have something in his saddlebags to start a fire. The spark and immediate flare of light confirmed her hopes. At least she'd have a chance to dry out while she figured out how to escape.

"Thank you." She stepped closer to the kneeling man. "I'm afraid of the dark," she whispered, hoping he'd believe her, though she lied through her teeth.

He tossed more wood on the small fire, but remained silent, his back to her. Maggie watched as the tiny flame licked the broken rungs and severed legs, growing larger and warmer, feeding on the dry wood.

Knowing he'd need more convincing before he believed she was afraid of the storm, she waited for the next flash before acting. As the eerie light showed in the dark outline of the cabin's only window, she gasped just loud enough to be heard. The man stiffened, then rose from his crouched position by the fire.

The thunder rumbled and she whimpered. He turned and walked slowly back toward her. "Nothing to fear."

That's what you think, me boy-o.

Maggie took a step backward before adopting a protective stance, wrapping her arms about her. She needed a distraction . . . she sent up a silent prayer for one. She had no sooner uttered the request than a gust of wind blew down the chimney, nearly blowing out the fire. He looked over his shoulder, cursed, and went back to tend the dying flames.

Maggie knew this was probably the best chance she'd have. She backed slowly toward the door, careful not to make a sound, pitifully grateful for the constant din of the storm. Out of the corner of her eye, she noticed a small cast-iron pan. Relief and a quick prayer of thanks swept through her, and she knew her plan *would* succeed.

She grabbed the pan and tiptoed over toward the man tending the fire. He'd already coaxed it back to life and was about to rise when she brought the heavy pan down onto the back of his head with all of the strength she could muster. He slumped into a heap on the floor at her feet.

For a heartbeat she just stood there staring in horrid fascination at his inert body, with her hands still wrapped around the handle of the pan. Drawing in one deep cleansing breath and then another, she steadied herself and remembered the documents . . . her room had been a shambles. Up until now, all she had been thinking of was getting away. There hadn't been time to even think about the papers.

Though it hadn't occurred to her right off, she knew now with a sinking feeling that the man had stolen her brother's papers. As far as she could remember, they hadn't stopped off anywhere along the way. If he took them, and she was sure he had, then he must still have them.

She didn't know how hard the man's head was, or how strong her blow, but the worry that he could come around at any moment was real. With that sobering thought foremost in mind, she dropped the pan.

Excruciating pain radiated across the top of her foot where the pan had landed. She closed her eyes and said one of her brother's favorite curses, then abruptly apologized for cursing.

Limping over to the saddlebags, she rifled through them.

Nothing.

Picking the wet leather saddlebags up, she upended them. Two pair of socks, a worn shirt, a pouch of chewing tobacco, and two boxes of bullets clattered to the floor. She watched the shells spill out of the squashed boxes and roll across the floor.

No papers.

A low moan made the tiny hairs on the back of her neck stand up. She was running out of time. She should leave now.

"I haven't come all this way and been skewered with a heathen's arrow only to give up now!"

Five minutes later, both bedrolls were open and spread out on the floor. Coffee, hardtack biscuits, beef jerky, and tins of beans lay piled on top of the bedding where she had dumped the sacks of supplies.

"Well, Maggie me girl . . . there is only one place ye haven't looked."

Jaw clenched, stomach churning, she walked over to the fallen man and knelt down on the floor. He was a large man, but his pockets did not look big enough to hide the leather folder. Inspiration hit like a blow between the eyes. They weren't in his pockets. He must have taken the papers out of the folder and hidden them.

She reached a hand toward his back pockets, then drew it back. The prospect of touching the man simply made her stomach turn over.

Inspiration hit. "His shirt!"

He moaned and stirred. No time to be squeamish.

She patted the back of his shirt . . . nothing. Scooting around him, Maggie reached a shaking hand toward his chest and lightly touched him. She felt the rolled-up wad of paper the second time she poked at his chest. Easing the roll sideways toward the placket of buttons, she pushed against the end nearest his underarm and moved it slowly toward the buttons.

The roll slid smoothly, then stopped.

She let a curse slip from between her tightly pressed lips. "I don't want to do this."

It took three tries before her hands quit shaking enough to open two shirt buttons and slide the roll of papers free. He groaned, louder this time, and shifted one of his legs.

She scooped the papers up and ran to the door. The muffled curse that erupted from behind her only spurred her onward. Wrenching the door open, she dashed out into the heart of the storm. Heedless of the nasty teeth the storm bared, she ran blindly into it. The wind whipped her hair into her eyes. Cold rain stung her cheeks, but she ran as if her life depended upon her speed. If things went her way, she would be able to run a good distance before he could catch up to her.

A loud thud and string of curses told her he found the pile of ruined supplies. "I hope he trips over them."

With only the lightning flashes to guide her way, it took longer than she hoped to find the trail. Worry nipped at her heels, while mud sucked at the toes of her brand-new high-button shoes. Lifting her skirts to keep from tripping became more and more difficult. Her green-and-white gingham dress was drenched, heavy with rainwater. Her lovely new shoes and dress would likely rot at the seams before the storm was finished making rags out of her clothes.

The storm eased enough for her to hear the unmistakable sounds of her pursuer crashing through the underbrush after her. The knowledge that he was close on her heels pushed her on when she was certain she couldn't go another step. The sudden sharp cramp in her side doubled her over. She grabbed it and pressed against the ache, her head swimming from lack of air. Gulping in deep breaths of cold air helped. After five or so, the ache was a little more bearable, enough to push on.

A shout from up ahead froze the blood in her veins. How could he have run past her and now be in front of her? The sound of other voices confused her for a moment, until she heard a vile curse and crash sound from somewhere behind her on the trail. Her captor was still behind her. Someone else was out in this dreadful storm. Her brain tried to reason out who would be desperate enough to be out on a night like this, but it was no use. Fear combined with exhaustion, making it impossible to string two thoughts together. But her faith was stronger than her fear. Putting her trust in that higher power, she ran like the devil was at her heels and threw back her head to scream.

Chapter Thirteen

J oshua blinked. "Maggie?"

The ghostly white form that ran toward him through the storm was definitely a woman. It had to be her. Forced to walk his horse through the worst of the downpour, he was already on foot. He dropped Blaze's reins and thought to meet her halfway, but she seemed to pick up speed the closer she got.

"Wait here," he told the weary search party.

"Is it Miss Flaherty?" Sheriff Coltrane asked.

Joshua did not have time to answer. He only had time to brace himself for the impact. Tensing his body, he opened his arms and caught the soggy wet bundle. Relief washed over him as he enveloped her in his arms.

"Maggie," he said, resting his head on the top of hers.

She shivered violently. "You're freezing." Concern for her, and the possibility of her kidnapper taking them by surprise, forced him to move. The powerful need to demand the reason she had for corresponding with James Ryan burned deep within him. He wanted to ask why she had traveled from New York to see the man. More than that, he needed to know what Ryan was to her. But his years as a lawman had him acting without the need to think, doing what needed to be done. He pulled her with him behind a stand of trees and scanned the area for signs of pursuit.

"Joshua," she whispered, wrapping her arms about his waist, resting her head against his back.

All thoughts of explanations and upholding the law dissolved at her touch. The woman he had tried so hard to forget was now holding onto him with a death grip. His heart pounded in his chest. The past few days spent worrying that he'd never find her had warred with the possibility that when he did, he would lose her to her intended. Suddenly neither possibility mattered. He pulled her around him until he could enfold her in his arms. When she melted into him, he sighed . . . Maggie was safe.

Worry was replaced by wonder, as her grip tightened around him. Possibilities replaced reasons as he reveled in the moment. Maggie had been found. She was all in one piece and clinging to him like a vine. But what about Ryan? his mind prodded.

With a will of iron, he reached behind him and took hold of her hands. Clasping them gently in his own, he rested them against his chest. His reason for being out in the midst of the storm faded. Drawing a deep breath did not clear his mind; it filled his senses with her sweet scent, reminding him of spring. Before she could befuddle his mind any further, he took a step back. His mind cleared. The distance definitely helped.

"I'm sorry for plowing into ye," Maggie said, staring down at her feet.

"What are you running from?" The voice to her right startled her.

Joshua realized Maggie did not know they were not alone.

"Merciful heavens," she said, looking at the group of men now standing in a semi-circle around her.

"Don't be afraid, Maggie," Joshua spoke reassuringly. "Sheriff Coltrane and these good men came with me all the way from Milford to find you."

Eyes wide with shock, she simply nodded her understanding.

"What are you running from?" Joshua asked.

"Who, not what."

"Who is it?" Joshua asked, trying to hang on to his rapidly dwindling patience. Standing so near to Maggie, not able to fully concentrate on the danger still at large, was irritating. But not knowing if he had the right to hold her was killing him.

"The man who stole me from me room."

"Stole you?" Sheriff Coltrane asked.

Joshua watched her expression change; she obviously had forgotten they were not alone. She nodded her head. "He tied me up and flung me across his lap like a sack of potatoes."

The waver in her voice told Joshua more than her words, as she recounted her tale of the kidnapping. Fear was a normal reaction to being abducted; he sensed she was trying to keep her fear under rigid control. He was sorry he had not been there to protect her and that she'd had to suffer the man's rough treatment of her.

"Coltrane, guard Maggie."

"I think—" the sheriff began.

"She'll be safer with you," he said cryptically.

"Joshua," she rasped, then paused. "Have a care, then."

He looked down at the heart-shaped face that had recently haunted his every waking hour. The depth of emotion on her face rocked him to the soles of his boots. Either she gave her heart easily, or she was reacting to the terror of her ordeal. Did he dare to hope she really cared for him? Either way, he could not afford to be swayed by her beauty now. Duty called. He nodded and turned to go.

"Split up," he ground out through clenched jaws, "and wait for my signal."

Making his way toward their quarry, Joshua focused on making as little sound as possible. He wanted to flush the man out and force him into the open. A whisper of a sound from behind him on the left had him pause midstride. Holding his breath, he waited. When he heard it a second time, he slipped the loop off his holster and slowly drew his Peacemaker, before slipping back toward the direction of the sound.

"Don't move," he ordered, sticking his gun into the small of the other man's back.

The man stiffened, but foolishly took another step forward.

Joshua pulled back the trigger on his gun, letting the unmistakable sound speak for him.

The man froze, dropped his gun, and slowly raised his hands high over his head.

He released the trigger and nudged the man again. "Bring 'em down real slow," he ordered, reaching for one wrist and bringing it around behind the man's broad back.

The man tensed and Joshua warned, "I wouldn't try it, unless you're anxious to see daylight through your shirtfront."

The instant the man's muscles relaxed, Joshua

wrenched his other arm around and snapped on the handcuffs. "Now walk."

The rest of the search party obviously heard the scuffle. They reappeared one by one.

"You ready to call it a night, Marshal?" one man called out.

"I sure could use a cup of coffee," another replied.

"Good work," Joshua said, and meant it. Six men could cover more ground faster than one man alone.

"Where's Maggie?" he asked, after scanning the spot where he'd left her in the sheriff's care.

"Over there," the sheriff answered. "Soon as you went off to find the kidnapper, she curled up against that rock over there, tucked her head onto her knees, and hasn't budged since."

Joshua stalked over toward the dark shape that appeared to be part of the large boulder. "She'll catch pneumonia sitting still in the wet like that. She's soaked to the skin."

He didn't even try to keep the concern from his words. Let them think what they would. He was too relieved that Maggie was safe to worry over his choice of words.

"I wrapped her in the piece of oilskin I found around your bedroll."

Joshua looked over his shoulder at the sheriff and nodded his head. "Sorry," he said slowly, and meant it.

She had him tied up in knots and acting before thinking. Neither action would help Maggie or himself.

"I'm done in," he offered by way of explanation. "We'd best mount up."

"What about him?" the sheriff asked, pointing toward the handcuffed man.

"Send one of your men back to find the horses."

"Will you wait here?"

Joshua shook his head no. "I'll head toward the Ryan

place; it's halfway between here and town. Miss Flaherty needs something dry to put on and something warm to fill her belly."

"Take two men with you," the sheriff said. "I'll send someone out to the ranch if I need you."

Joshua walked over toward Maggie and for a moment just stood there looking down at her. Rain splashed in the puddles pooling around the rock, and the woman huddled against it. He could ignore the cool drops that spattered against his face and neck, but it was beyond his power to ignore the woman who had come into his well-ordered life and turned it upside-down.

Regret sifted through feelings of hurt and confusion. What would he do if she truly was spoken for? Did he dare try to sway her feelings away from Ryan? He shook his head. No, that wouldn't be right. He wasn't some young hothead who couldn't control his trigger finger or his heart. Besides, he owed it to Maggie to respect her wishes. He had no one to blame but himself for allowing himself to be attracted, then distracted, by her.

Kneeling in the mud, he scooped the woman and the tarp into his arms. Her soft sigh was music to his ears. The way she snuggled closer against his chest warmed the cold spot over his heart. Maggie was attracted to him; he'd swear to that fact on a stack of Bibles. But had she given her heart? How soon before he could work up the courage to ask her flat-out? Depending upon her answer, he'd stake a claim of his own, or saddle up and ride off into the sunset.

Maggie woke feeling groggy, but warm and secure. The rocking motion kept her from waking fully. A rhythmic thud softly pounded beneath her right cheek. She signed deeply, unable to remember the last time she'd felt so protected, so safe.

Joshua.

The last thing she could clearly recall was being held in his strong arms. She opened one eye partway and looked up through her lashes. Dawn was breaking and with it the storm clouds. Relief spread through her like a balm rubbed on sore muscles. All the worry of the past few days shriveled up and died. *I'm safe, so long as I'm right here in his arms.* She was about to ask him how long he planned to stay on in town, when he spoke to someone.

"Go knock on the door. See if you can rouse anyone."

The sound of spurs jingling and boot heels thudding against the ground told her two things. They were not alone, and they had reached a destination of some sort.

She was about to open both eyes, when Joshua surprised her by pulling her closer and brushing his warm lips against the top of her head. Her whole scalp tingled in response to the caress.

"Why, Maggie?"

The strangled sound of his voice made her heart pound and her mind race to understand him. Why what? Before she could figure out what he was talking about, the sound of a door slamming and boot heels pounding on wood startled her.

"Maggie?" a very familiar gruff voice called out. "Maggie, me darlin'!"

Seamus! Before she could speak, she was hauled from Joshua's arms and wrapped tightly in a hug that threatened to rob her lungs of air and snap every one of her ribs.

"You've come! I knew you wouldn't let me down," her brother exclaimed, whirling her around in his arms.

"Me head's spinnin', ye overgrown beast. Put me down!"

She laughed, cuffing the side of his head affectionately. Her brother stopped spinning and pulled her back against the wide expanse of his sleep-warmed chest. He placed a noisy kiss on both of her cheeks, before she could fully catch her breath.

"Let me down."

"So this is yer Maggie?" a tall well-built man with hair as red as her own said, walking toward her.

"Aye," Seamus answered, "my very own." He set her on her feet, and wrapped a hand about her waist.

The sudden sound of a horse riding away had her craning her head around in time to see Joshua urge his horse to a flat out gallop. Her heart lurched at the sight of his broad back disappearing into the misty light of dawn. Disbelief had her rubbing her fists in her eyes. He was leaving!

The joy of her reunion with her brother faded until a dull achy feeling crept up from her toes and settled in her stomach. Despair coiled around her heart and pulled taut. She had the awful premonition that she'd never see Marshal Turner again. The very thought of never looking into those grass-green eyes, never sweeping her fingertips across his handsome features again, made her lightheaded. But the prospect of never being held against his broad chest, never being able to hear the steady beat of his heart, made her heart clench in pain. Not since Rory died had she felt such an overwhelming sorrow. She felt the emptiness to the depths of her soul.

"Maggie," her brother said, focusing on the group of men waiting on the porch steps. "You must be exhausted. Come inside, I'd like you to meet the men who've slaved alongside me to build all that you see." The pride in her brother's voice was unmistakable.

Maggie didn't know if she could hide the feelings running riot in her breast. The marshal's desertion and rejection had opened up the door to emotions she had kept safely locked away for years. But she had to try to appear normal, for her brother's sake.

" 'Tis a fine job ye've done, lads," she said, acknowledging each man with a quivering smile.

Only one man seemed to notice her smile did not reach her eyes. His gaze flickered toward the rapidly shrinking form of the man who rode like the devil was chasing him.

Maggie started when the silent man turned to look at her. The livid scar slashing across his cheek still looked painful. "Who did this to ye?" she asked, touching her fingertips to his chin.

"Rustlers," Seamus answered for the man.

"I may be able to fix something to ease the pain," she offered, looking over her shoulder one last time. But Joshua was gone. Not even the cloud of dust his racing horse raised remained. A wave of cold swept through her, making her shudder.

Why hadn't she taken the time to thank him? she wondered. Because he'd gone after the kidnapper, she reasoned. But then why hadn't she said good-bye? Why hadn't *he?*

Seamus. She'd traveled more miles than she'd care to count bringing the proof of the ranch's ownership to her brother. It was time to focus on the reason for her being in Emerson.

"Maggie, you're shivering!"

The concern in her brother's voice brought unwanted tears to her eyes. She blinked them away.

"I had a bit of a time last night," she said, stumbling when a stabbing pain shot through the left side of her face from jaw to crown.

"Here now, lass. Let me help—"

She reached out to grab hold of the hand a dark-haired man held out to her, and winced at the loudly uttered curse that fell from his lips. The horror in the man's voice had her straightening to her feet and looking over her shoulder to see what worried him so.

Someone tugged on her hands, snapping her attention back to the men on the porch.

"What are ye—" The words died in her throat at the sight of her raw wrists. "Well now, that explains the stingin'."

"Maggie, you're bleeding!"

Her brother sounded as if he would weep over that fact.

"I'll be fine," she said softly, cupping the side of his face in her hand.

"Jamie . . . her face—" a red-headed man rasped.

"Well now, I didn't have a chance to clean meself up. If ye'll point me toward the soap and a bit of warm water—" Her brother grabbed her by the upper arms, cutting off her words.

"Who hit you?" he demanded in a deadly voice that promised retribution.

"No one, I—"

"I want the man's name."

"If ye must know the whole of it, can I sit down through the tellin'?"

"Come with me, lass," the bull of a man with dark hair said, holding out his arm to her.

Reacting to the kindness and display of manners, Maggie gave him her arm and let him lead her into the kitchen. Let her brother follow or not, as he chose. What little energy she felt after seeing him, slipped away, leaving her feeling ready to drop.

"Sean! Is there hot water for tea?" Seamus snapped out, as he entered the kitchen behind them and glared down at her.

She shifted under her brother's scrutiny, straightening in the chair until she no longer slumped.

"Only coffee, we've no tea."

"Flynn—bring that pitcher of water over."

"Mick, lad—"

A tall gangly boy walked into the kitchen from the darkened hallway and stopped in front of Maggie. Without asking, he took her hands in his and studied the battered flesh on her wrists, then looked up and studied her face.

"Me ma used to have marks like this on her," he said quietly, gently lowering her hands back into her lap.

"I used to believe her when she told me she'd fallen, or caught her hand—"

The poor boy's Adam's apple bobbed up and down, he was trying so hard not to show any emotion in front of the men. Maggie swallowed the lump of sympathy she'd felt constrict her throat at the boy's words. He and his mother must have lived through some very hard times.

"Who did this to you, ma'am?" he asked.

"It happened when I was bound, gagged, and tossed over a packhorse like a sack of potatoes," she said with a sigh.

"Me head kept knockin' against somethin' hard . . . I'm thinkin' now it may have been the skillet . . . it was a long ride to the cabin."

"Cabin?" Seamus ground out, looking for all the world as if he were primed for a fight.

"Let her finish," the dark-haired man interrupted.

"Aye, Reilly."

Maggie turned toward the man who had coaxed her into the ranch house. "John Reilly?"

"Aye."

"I've met someone who remembers ye fondly . . . and

offered me a sip of the Irish ye traded for winter supplies a few years back."

"Taylor Smith," Reilly said softly.

"I was stayin' with them after I'd been shot—"

"Shot? You were shot?" Seamus thundered, coming to his feet.

"What happened?" the red-headed man her brother called Flynn asked.

"Let's get some whiskey in the lass before we try to pry any more words out of her," Reilly suggested.

Maggie forced a smile, though her jaw ached. "I'll need to be knowin' the rest of yer names before I lift a glass with the likes of ye."

"John Reilly, ye know." Her brother nodded toward the stocky dark-haired man.

Maggie smiled.

"Michael Flynn has hair red as yer own."

Her gaze shifted to a tall rangy man with hair red as fire.

"Mine's not that bright."

"Aye, lass," her brother said, grinning, "every bit as bright. Thomas and Sean Murphy," he continued, pointing toward two chestnut-haired, freckle-faced men who stood by the back door.

"William Masterson, whom ye've promised to fix the salve for."

"I've just the thing in me bag. . . ." The rest of what she was going to say was lost, as she remembered her bag was still in the back room at the Smiths' in Milford. "No matter, I can fix up a new batch; no doubt the rest of ye can use it."

"Thank you, Maggie," the solemn man standing beside her brother said, his dark eyes searching her face before he looked away.

"Travis Brennan," Seamus said, acknowledging the only light-haired man in the group.

He must have slipped in while she was not paying attention, she thought, then her heart lurched. The man had pale blond locks—but he wasn't Joshua.

"Mick . . . Michael O'Toole's the lad fetching the glasses," Seamus added. "He and his mother will be staying with us for a time."

Maggie decided to prod that story out of her brother later. Right now she was weary to the bone, and grateful for the whiskey. After drinking half the potent amber liquid, she looked up at the solemn faces that surrounded her and quietly began to retell all that had happened to her over the last few days since arriving in Colorado.

The telling of her tale was hard enough, but their endless questions exhausted her. While she relayed the story, a bowl of warm water and sliver of soap appeared on the table in front of her. She moved to pick up the soap thinking to care for her wrists, but to her surprise her brother knelt beside her chair and began to bathe her sore wrists with exquisite care.

Maggie let the pain wash over her, but did not outwardly acknowledge it, knowing it would worry her brother.

While he slowly worked up a lather, Mick laid out a few strips of linen that smelled of sunshine and fresh air.

"I've a salve the doctor left here, the last time Flynn—"

"No need to tell the lass everything," Flynn grumbled.

"I'm near dead on me feet, Seamus—" she began, trying to distract her brother from continuing with a story that obviously embarrassed the poor man. She'd pry the story from Reilly's lips later, watching the way a broad grin lit the man's face. From the looks on Flynn and Reilly's faces, it would be a tale worth repeating.

"Why do ye call him Seamus?" Reilly asked.

" 'Tis his given name," she answered, confused by the question.

" 'Tis James," one of the Murphy brothers corrected her, while the man beside him nodded his agreement.

"Aye . . . or Jamie," Masterson offered.

She looked over at her brother. He ran a hand through his hair, twice. She knew then that something was wrong. Though it had been a few years since she had seen him, she remembered his habit of raking his hands through his hair when he was deeply troubled.

Waiting until he finished bathing the side of her face, she asked, "What is it, Seamus?"

"Ye need a bath, lass."

"Are ye offering to heat the water?"

He shook his head yes, then answered her earlier question. "I did what I had to do. Don't ye see?"

"No," she said, shaking her head. "Why don't ye tell me?"

"Remember how hard it was for Da to find work when we first arrived?" he asked, his brow furrowed.

"Aye."

"The signs saying Irish need not apply? The hired muscle who beat Da?"

She nodded. It had been a bad time. So many hopes for starting over in a new land, free from famine and disease. The shock of arriving and having to face a whole new set of prejudices against them, for the same old reasons—who and what they were—would never be forgotten. Although their mother had tried to get them to work on the forgiving part.

" 'Tis not half as bad as it was traveling West," he finished, looking down at the hands he clasped and unclasped.

She reached over and twined her fingers with his. "If

it would ease the tellin'," she offered, "I'll forgive ye now for somethin' I've no doubt plagues ye."

The look of gratitude that filled his deep blue eyes warmed her heart.

"I've changed me name."

"And what's wrong with Seamus?" she asked, her temper beginning to rise.

"I thought she said she'd forgive him?" one of the men asked loudly.

"I did," she snapped back. "But yer name . . ."

"I did what I had to do."

She raked a hand through her tangled hair, in a gesture so like her older brother that the group of men around her smiled. She thought they were daft. "All right," she conceded. "Ye did what needed to be done."

He nodded. The other men nodded in unison.

"What'll I call ye then?"

"James," he answered quickly. " 'Tis the Americanization of Seamus."

"Well, in that case—"

"James Ryan."

"Well, at least ye've kept yer middle name," she said, unable to keep the hurt from her voice.

"Do ye think I'd give up me name, turn me back on Da, if I had another choice?" he demanded, rising to his feet.

Maggie rose to her feet and wrapped her arms tightly about his waist. Placing her head against his chest, she sighed. "Forgive me for seemin' to doubt ye, I—"

The tears that she'd bottled up inside her, from the moment she'd received his telegram, choked her.

His big hand stroked her hair. "Maggie darlin', I've a fearful temper."

She tightened her grip, wanting to tell him that her

temper was far worse, but she couldn't speak past the lump in her throat.

"You're safe now, darlin'," her brother soothed. "Go ahead and cry."

Safe? She'd felt safe in Joshua's arms. But she didn't know if she'd ever see him again. It couldn't be her destiny to be rescued by the same man twice, and never see him again, could it? Just the thought of it cracked the invisible dam she'd erected to hold her fears and feelings at bay when Rory died.

Her brother murmured to her in their native tongue. The musical sound of the Gaelic flowing softly around her soothed her. And though it was Seamus's arms wrapped around her, she closed her eyes and imagined it was Joshua who held her close, protecting her.

But he's gone.

The one man who might have been able to heal the rend in her heart left by Rory's death, had ridden away without a word of good-bye. She knew in her heart that she'd lost the only other chance she would ever have at love.

The crack around her heart widened, and her tears poured out.

Chapter Fourteen

"**M**aggie love," her brother whispered, gathering her into his arms.

One by one the men filed out of the room, until they were alone.

" 'Tisn't because I need you to call me James, is it?" he asked.

Maggie shook her head against the broad expanse of her brother's chest. She inhaled the clean soap scent of him and relaxed against him. The realization that her brother's chest was nearly as heavily muscled as a certain marshal's brought on a fresh spurt of tears.

"I can't go back to the way things were," he explained. "Even if I could, everyone around here knows me as James."

" 'Tisn't yer name," she cried, struggling to get control of herself.

"I promise to find the man who hurt you and I'll tear a strip off his hide—"

Maggie could not hold back her snort of laughter.

"Are you cryin' or laughin'?" her brother asked, his brogue thickening. A clear tip-off that he was vexed with her.

"Oh Sea . . . James. I'm just tired."

"Does the arrow wound still pain you?"

She shook her head.

"Was Marshal Turner the man who helped ye?"

"Aye," she said, her voice going soft. "He's a brave man, with hands as big as yourself and Da's."

"Have you feelings for the man, then?" he asked quietly, tightening his hold on her.

Maggie pulled back from his embrace and wiped the backs of her hands over her cheeks, and under her eyes. "And what if I do?" she challenged. She'd not had to answer to anyone for the last five years, and she'd not start now.

"As your older brother, and only living male relative—"

"Stop right there," she said, poking her index finger in the middle of his chest. "I've handled me own affairs since Da passed on, and Ma's as well, until . . ."

"Aye, Maggie," he said gently, taking a hold of her hand. "You did just grand, but now that you're here, won't you let me share some of your burden?"

"I might," she said, relenting. "But just now, I'd like to lie down, just for a wee bit, mind," she said, shaking her finger in his face until he grinned at her. "Wake me in a few hours so I can make a proper meal for the lot of ye."

"You'll rest today."

"I'll not."

"Maggie."

"Jamie," she said, drawing out her brother's name, hoping by compromising on the use of his name, he'd agree to let her take over in the kitchen.

"If you wake up on your own, then I might let you ask Sean if he minds if you take his turn cooking."

"Ye won't be sorry," she said, relieved that he'd almost agreed. "I've been wantin' to make a couple of Ma's pies."

"Apple pie?"

Maggie could tell from the look on her brother's face that he might be persuaded to let her bake a few pies. Back in Ireland, he'd polish off a pie for breakfast all by himself, if their mother didn't catch him first.

"Well then, you'd best rest up, lass," he said, taking her by the arm and leading her upstairs.

She slept like the dead for the rest of the day and on through the night.

Maggie woke with a start and sat up straight. Her heart was pounding and her skin moist from perspiration. The demons from her nightmare vanished the moment she'd opened her eyes, but the memory of what she'd dreamed lingered.

Her hands ached. She looked down at them and nearly laughed out loud. They were white-knuckled, fisted about the bedsheets.

"It was a dream," she said aloud to banish the wisp of the dream that lingered about her. But the image of the blond-haired man cradled in her arms haunted her. She could still see the life begin to dim in his beautiful green eyes. Though she'd tried to save him, the outlaw's aim had been true.

"Don't weep for me mo croi, my heart. Promise me you'll not bury your love beside me."

She shook her head and looked about her. The windows had flour-sack curtains tied back with bits of frayed twine, not the soft white curtains her mother had lovingly trimmed with bits of the lace their grandmother had crocheted.

She was in Colorado . . . not Ireland, though the dying man's words were no dream. Rory had made her promise to live and love again.

"Why then did I dream that Joshua was the one who died in me arms?"

It must be a warning, she thought. If she gave her love to him he would die too. Heaven help her, she didn't know what to do. She couldn't reason it out.

Dragging herself from the bed, although she ached in a dozen places, was better than lying in bed slipping back into the nightmare.

Grateful for the pitcher of fresh water and clean cloth, she washed as best she could, promising herself to ask her brother about a bath later. There was breakfast to see to and pies promised, and a poultice to prepare for William's injury.

An hour later, she was rolling out piecrust, careful not to get any on the bandages on her wrists; two trays of biscuits were cooling and two more were in the oven. Crisply fried bacon was piled high on a platter with thin slices of ham. The frying eggs needed tending. After the idleness of her journey West and the enforced bedrest, it felt good to be doing something useful. Her arm ached, but she wasn't going to share that little tidbit with anyone just yet. She'd finish her pies first, she decided. Placing the bottom crust in the pie tin, she filled it with the apples, sugar, and cinnamon. She placed the flattened bit of crust on top and began to flute the edges.

Finished, she drew in a deep breath and sniffed. The warm yeasty scent of buttermilk biscuits baking was soothing. Like home. She opened the oven, took out the trays, and put the pies in.

"What smells like heaven and cinnamon?"

"William," she said, jolting in surprise, wondering why she hadn't heard the big man walk up behind her.

He smiled, closed his eyes, and drew in a deep breath. "We've not had any sweets since Sean tried his hand at making biscuits." He smiled. "It smells of home."

"Where is home?"

She watched his smile turn upside-down. "Far from here, lass."

His silence seemed uneasy. Rather than intrude, she bid him to sit at the table while she applied the poultice she'd prepared from the comfrey root she'd found with the salve the doctor had left behind for whatever ailed Flynn.

"Have ye had no sweets at all?" She wiped her hands on her apron and smoothed the hair from his brow.

"None."

"You poor man," she sympathized. "Not even a decent scone?"

He shook his head looking so like a lost little boy deprived of his treats, she had to smile. "Well then, I hope ye like apple pie."

His eyes sparkled, and his grin widened. "I plan on having more than one piece, just to make sure—"

"Biscuits!" Reilly called out, coming in through the back door.

"Why didn't ye bang on a pot or ring the bell if break-fast was ready."

"Jamie!" Reilly hollered out the door.

"Coming!"

"You'd think the lot of you hadn't eaten in days," she said with a smile.

"It's been a week since we've had decent biscuits."

"Longer since we've had anything sweet."

"And Lordy, do I crave something sweet!"

"Well, don't just stand there!" she said to the group of men gathered about her, her hands on her hips. "Yer breakfast is gettin' cold."

"Maggie, you look tired," James said, coming to stand beside her.

She tried to shoo him away and heft the platter herself, but he took it right out of her hands and motioned for her to get the coffeepot. The group of normally talkative Irishmen was silent, except for a sigh or two of pure pleasure, as they put away every last bit of food she'd prepared.

"Jamie," she said, touching her brother's broad shoulder, "I forgot to give ye these last night." Reaching into the deep pocket of her apron, she pulled out the roll of papers she'd traveled so far to deliver. She placed them into her brother's hands.

They shook as he carefully unrolled them. "Ahh, Maggie darlin' . . . when you didn't say anything about them last night, I was afraid to ask. But I knew I could depend on you."

The break in her brother's voice brought tears to her eyes. "Well then, I'll just go up and see how yer guest is doin'. Oh," she said, turning back, "do ye mind if I borrow the wagon?"

"Wherever you need to go, one of the men can drive you."

"I'd rather see to me errands meself."

Five pair of eyes turned toward her brother, waiting for him to either agree or disagree with her request. She held her breath and waited.

"You've been through so much, can't you let someone drive you?"

"I didn't want to take anyone away from their duties,"

she said, wringing her hands, her nerves taut as a bow-string.

"William?" James asked.

"No problem. I just have a bit of the fence repair left to finish and then I'll be free."

"Well then," Maggie said, rubbing her damp hands on her apron. "Ye know where to find me."

William pulled the team to a stop in front of the Bank of Emerson and set the brake. "I'll wait outside if you like."

Maggie nodded. "I won't be long," she promised, walking through the glass-front door to the bank.

"May I help you?" the short spindly man who hovered near the entrance asked.

"Yes. I would like to see Mr. Emerson. I need to have money transferred from me bank back home in New York."

The man bowed and made his way across the open lobby to the narrow hallway just beyond. While she watched, he knocked on the frosted glass door and waited for the summons to enter.

Uneasy at the prospect of meeting the man who single-handedly owned and ran the town, she let her gaze take in the compact room. The floor was scrupulously clean, and the walls painted a soft green. It was not quite on par with the bank she was used to doing business with back in New York, but for a frontier town, it was quite nice.

"May I help you?" a booming voice called out from behind her.

"Mr. Emerson," she said, "I'm Margaret Mary Flah-erty."

The flash of surprise, followed by an unreadable glint in the rotund man's eyes, unnerved her. While she calmly explained what she needed, she noticed something in the man's gaze that seemed sinister, almost malevolent. The feeling passed as the man came forward, hand extended, to greet her.

Nerves, she thought.

"If you'll just come right this way, Miss Flaherty," he said, ushering her toward his office at the rear of the bank. "We can conduct our business in private."

For some reason, the proprietary touch of his hand at her waist made her skin crawl. She shivered involuntarily, but he didn't seem to notice. He opened the door to his office, motioning for her to precede him.

Once she was seated, he asked, "What may I do for you?"

"I need to send a wire to my bank in New York City to transfer funds," she said, striving for a congenial tone.

"That will not be a problem," he said solicitously. "I'll need the name of the bank, your account number, and the amount you wish to transfer."

After handling the details, she felt better. She was now prepared to return the money her brother had so generously sent to her at a time when she was certain he needed it more. She wanted it to be a surprise, while at the same time she was determined to see that he accepted the money.

After signing the appropriate documents, she looked up and caught the man's glare of anger. It changed quickly to one of indifference. Her instincts had not been wrong. She had not imagined the dark feelings emanating from the man.

"I'll see to this immediately," he said, rising.

Obviously her cue to do the same, so she rose to her feet. "Thank you for your time," she said, though it pained her to keep the smile plastered on her face.

All the way back to the ranch, she wondered what

reason the banker could have for his dislike of her. But the only reason she could come up with was the fact that she was an immigrant. She had received similar treatment before. After all this time, it shouldn't bother her, but it did. She didn't even know the man, but she was long used to the disdain from those who considered themselves to be the upper class—the wealthy.

On the ride back to the ranch, she could feel William's eyes on her, but rather than ask what he thought, she kept her feelings of unease and distress to herself. Instead she focused on looking forward to losing herself in the routine of cooking for the men who stuck with James through good times and bad.

Hugh Emerson's hands clenched and unclenched for the third time while he stared down at the name before him.

The woman had been here, seated right across from him, but he could do nothing. He had no choice but to let her go.

"The wrong woman," he rasped.

The gunman he sent to Milford to take care of Ryan's sister had shot the wrong woman!

"She has red hair," he grumbled. "Freckles. She's short and plump!"

"Maggie?" Mick called out, running toward her as William was helping her down out of the wagon.

"Is everything all right?" she asked, as the young man stopped to catch his breath.

"I'm so glad you're back—it's my ma . . . she's burning up."

Hastily thanking William for taking her to town, Maggie hurried into the house after Mick. The door to the room his mother was using stood open. She followed him inside.

"Open the window, like a good lad," she asked him, while she laid a hand to the frail-looking woman's brow. Her skin felt dry and hot.

"I'll need ye to fetch some clean cloths from the cupboard in the kitchen and cool water from the pump for me."

He ran to do her bidding and was back before she could wonder how long it would take him. "There's a good lad," she said softly.

Maggie dipped a length of cloth in the cool water and wrung out most of the water before smoothing it across the pale woman's brow. Turning the cloth over, Maggie smoothed it across the pale woman's cheeks and neck, drawing out more heat. While she continued the motions of wetting the cloth and wringing it out, Mick watched her every move.

"Can ye tell Jamie I'll be late starting the noon meal?"

"But me ma—"

"Will be just fine," she assured him, motioning for him to go and do her bidding.

"Who are you?" a raspy voice asked, calling Maggie's attention back to her patient.

"I'm Jamie's sister."

"Maggie?"

"Aye," she said softly. "I guess he's been waitin' for me."

"He's been worried."

"Can ye sit up? I'll give ye a bit of water."

Maggie helped her sit up and take a drink.

"Mrs. O'Toole—"

"Please, call me Bridget."

"Bridget, have ye had this fever long?"

She shook her head.

Maggie noticed the unhealthy pallor to Bridget's skin, and the dark smudges beneath her eyes. Besides that, the poor woman seemed to be wasting away, nothing but skin and bones. An idea came to Maggie. Though she'd not seen the ravages of starvation firsthand, she'd listened to each and every story of those who had.

"When was the last time ye ate yer fill?"

The woman looked away from her. Maggie guessed if Bridget had not been flushed with fever, the woman would have flushed with guilt.

"Young Mick is the picture of health," Maggie said slowly, pretending to try to reason out what she'd already surmised.

"Aye, he looks so much like his Da...." Bridget turned to look at Maggie. "I don't suppose I'm fooling anyone but myself," she said tiredly. "Am I?"

"Me own parents would have starved themselves, if it meant me brother and I would not go hungry. I'm not goin' to tell ye ye've made a mistake, when I'd do the same if Mick was me own."

"Thank you for understanding," Bridget said slowly. "The doctor doesn't agree with me. He refused to see me again, unless I start eating more." Her voice sounded strangled. "But I've gone so long without, I can't eat without getting sick to my stomach."

"At least I know what to do. Me parents lived through the worst of the famine back in Ireland," she said, looking out the window. "They were luckier than most."

"I've heard tales, such sad stories of waste and want," Bridget said softly, reaching a hand out to Maggie.

Maggie grasped the thin hand in her own and squeezed it gently. "We'll start with a bit of bread soaked in broth, at little at a time, five to six times a day."

"But I can't eat—"

"Ye will, I know ye can. Trust me to help ye."

Bridget nodded her head.

"First we have to cool ye down and get some water back into ye. I'll make up some strong tea . . . I forgot, we have no tea."

"Mick can go to town for some."

"Maggie?" she heard her brother call from downstairs.

"Aye, coming."

She gave Bridget another few sips of water, then helped her to lie back down. "Ye must rest now. I'll be back with the bread and broth."

"How can I thank you or Jamie?"

Jamie is it? she thought.

"Not at all," she said. "I'll be back after I see to their meal."

On the way down the stairs, she smiled to herself. Her brother was in for a shock when his houseguest started putting on weight. If her guess was right, once Bridget's cheeks filled back out and her color came back, she'd dazzle Jamie with her beauty. But more than that, the woman obviously had feelings for her brother. *Poor man,* she thought with a laugh. Maggie rubbed her hands together, anticipating the day when her big brother was knocked off his feet by the frail beauty upstairs.

Chapter Fifteen

Right after the mid-day meal the following day, she heard loud voices coming from the barn. She poked her head out the back door and listened.

"Where's Ryan?" a familiar deep voice demanded.

Joshua!

Forgetting everything but the fact that he'd come back, she picked up her skirts and ran down the steps, nearly tripping over her own feet to get to the barn.

"He's in town," she heard Reilly answer.

"I need to speak to him—"

"Joshua!" Maggie called out, her breath clogging in her lungs after one look at him. Heaven help her, she was desperate for him to look at her.

He nodded at her, but she couldn't see his face. The angle of sun, and the brim of his hat, hid most of his face in shadows.

His stiff stance told her something was wrong. "Can I help—"

"I need to speak to Ryan," he said brusquely.

His tone hurt. The fact that he wouldn't look at her wounded her deeply. With all that had passed between them, she couldn't just let it go. "He's paying a call on—"

"I don't have time to be sociable."

As if that said it all, he turned his back on her.

Maggie drew in a breath to cover the anguished moan that almost slipped past her guard. She would not give the man the satisfaction of knowing how much his rejection hurt her. He threw all that she wanted to offer back in her face, treating her like a complete stranger! Destiny or not, a woman could only take so much. Stiffening her spine, Maggie turned back toward the house, her chin held high, her heart in pieces.

Joshua heard Maggie's retreating footsteps, but didn't trust himself to turn around and watch her walk away.

"No need to be cruel, Marshal," Reilly said, scowling at him.

"I have a job to do—"

"If ye weren't trying to help Jamie find the rustlers, I'd knock yer teeth down yer throat."

Joshua eyed the shorter man, taking in the breadth of the man's stocky frame. Going up against Reilly would be like hitting a brick wall, he thought, but worth it if it would help him blow off the frustration that had been dogging his heels since he'd watched James Ryan sweep Maggie into his arms. He had a job to do, which now included finding out who was behind the attempt on Maggie's life, and her kidnapping, before he could allow himself to think about a future with the distracting woman.

"Magg—Miss Flaherty mentioned that her brother Seamus was having difficulty with Emerson over at the bank, similar to Ryan. I need to speak to him about it. I think I can use Flaherty as another claim against Emerson."

The look on Reilly's face changed from anger to astonishment, then wonder. "I don't think ye can use Flaherty."

"If I can find him, I know I can convince him to add his claims to Ryan's."

Reilly looked over at Maggie's retreating form and shook his head. "Ye can't use Flaherty's claim as another against Emerson."

"Why not? If Emerson is trying to pull the same game on more than one man—"

"Ryan is Maggie's brother."

"Maggie's brother's name is Seamus," Joshua said slowly, wondering why the man who worked for Ryan could be so confused.

"Aye, and Seamus is Gaelic for James."

"James," Joshua whispered. "Then Ryan's not Maggie's intended?"

Reilly gave a shout of laughter. "He may love his sister, but he's a fine upstandin' Christian man, and don't hold to no—"

But Joshua had already jumped down off his horse and headed toward the ranch house at a dead run.

"Maggie!" he called, as he hit the bottom step of the porch.

The kitchen door banged shut on his hand, as he tried to slip through, creasing three fingers. He swore under his breath and pushed against the dead weight holding the door shut.

"Maggie, let me in!" he demanded. But the door wouldn't budge. She must have been pushing hard against the door to keep it closed.

"Maybe Miss Flaherty doesn't want you bothering her," a voice called out from behind him. He didn't need to turn around to find out who stood behind him. It didn't matter which one of Ryan's men stood there, he wasn't leaving until he'd talked to Maggie, face to face. The wooden barrier between them would not keep him from her. He needed to touch her. His hands started to shake anticipating it. Joshua was man enough to admit he was desperate to hold her.

"She will once she hears what I have to say."

"I don't have time to be sociable, Marshal Turner!" came Maggie's muffled reply. Her weight still held the door closed. One quick shove and it would open, but he didn't want to do that. He wanted her to open the door and let him in.

"Seems to me like she's not interested."

"I can handle this meself, William!"

The door was slowly opening, even though he could tell she was putting all of her body weight against it. She was weakening.

"Maggie, let me in," he asked softly. "I need to talk to you about Seamus."

"What's me brother got to do with anything?"

His patience snapped the same moment the thought struck him . . . her brother! Her connection to James Ryan was the reason behind the attempted murder and kidnapping! He closed his eyes and said a silent prayer of thanks. Now that he knew what direction to go in, he could concentrate on the problem at hand . . . Margaret Mary Flaherty.

He wouldn't wait to be asked. He'd be an old man if he did. The sound of her feet sliding across the floor as he muscled the door open was deeply gratifying. She'd soon learn how to control that fiery temper of hers. If she didn't, it would be his pleasure to teach her how to rein it in.

"Marshal!" he heard Reilly calling him, but he ignored him.

"Why didn't you tell me Seamus is your brother?" Joshua advanced slowly, backing her into a corner until she had no choice but to tip her head back and look up at him.

"What of it?"

"And James Ryan, who is he to you?"

Maggie tilted her head at him, narrowed her eyes and lifted her chin in a defiant stance. "Why should ye care?"

"Ahh, Maggie," Joshua said softly. "I've been trying to stay away from you, but I can't. I've tried to put you from my mind and concentrate on my job—but I can't."

He reached out and snagged one of her hands.

"Ye've done a fine job of it, Marshal," she bit out, trying to pull her hand out of his.

"I thought Ryan was your intended."

"But he's me brother!"

He watched the murderous glint in her eyes soften. He held both of her hands in his, and gently rubbed his thumbs across her palms. He felt a shudder go through her. He stroked her palms again. She shuddered again. He almost grinned.

"I thought you were traveling West to be married."

"To me brother? Are ye daft?" Maggie's eyes were round with shock.

"I didn't know James was Seamus," he said quietly, pulling her into his arms.

"Marshal, Ryan's gone into town," Reilly called out from the back porch.

Maggie resisted at first. He expected it. He didn't add

any more pressure, but held firm until he heard her sigh, and felt her melt into his embrace.

"I almost lost my mind, when he wrapped you in his arms, calling you his Maggie," he confessed, nuzzling his face in her silken hair.

"But I am his Maggie—his sister Maggie. . . ." She laid her head against his chest.

It felt so right, having her lean against him.

"I know we haven't known each other long," he said, pressing another kiss to the top of her head. He breathed deeply, unable to resist drawing in her sweet scent. Lavender and rain would always remind him of the long ride back to the ranch with her bundled in his arms.

"The first time we met, I was drawn to you." He kissed her forehead.

"Your courage was beyond anything I'd imagined a woman could possess." He placed a kiss on the tip of her nose.

"He's going to confront Emerson with his proof," Reilly said, bursting into the kitchen, startling them apart.

Joshua hugged Maggie hard against him for a heart-beat while his brain changed gears, and he focused on the danger Ryan faced if he confronted Emerson on the banker's own territory.

He slowly nodded. "How long has he been gone?"

"Only a half hour or so," Reilly answered.

"Is Jamie in trouble?" Maggie asked, taking a step back from his arms.

"I know a shortcut to town," Masterson called out from the open door. "I'll ride with you."

"I'd rather you stayed to guard Maggie."

"You don't know Emerson," Masterson ground out. "You'll need a man you can trust at your back."

Joshua groaned. He knew he was out of time, so he relented. "Let's go."

"Joshua!" Maggie called out as she followed behind him.

He paused, one foot in the stirrup about to swing up into the saddle.

"Be careful," she urged him, laying a hand to his knee. "I—"

The sound of shots being fired suddenly galvanized him into action. He settled in the saddle and pulled his rifle out with one hand and his Colt with the other. Both weapons were cocked and ready to fire when five men came riding up the lane, guns blazing.

"Get down!" Joshua shouted to Maggie.

He saw her hit the ground out of the corner of his eye, then wheeled his horse to face the men racing toward them. This was it, the first test. He would not fail Maggie. He planned on spending the rest of his life protecting her, holding her . . . loving her.

With a single-mindedness that had seen him through more than one ambush, he took aim and shot the gun right out of one man's hand.

Then he winged another, and started aiming for a third, when he heard a rifle being fired from somewhere behind him.

The man he was aiming for fell out of his saddle and hit the ground. He didn't stop to see who had fired. He needed to concentrate on his next target, the big man who had been riding at the center of the group.

Once he had the man in his sights, he began to fire off one shot after another with his Winchester. The man's hat flew off his head, then Joshua took aim and peppered the ground in front of the gunman's horse. The black beast reared back on his hind legs and threw his rider from the saddle.

In the quiet that followed, Joshua took stock of the situation. Reilly and Masterson had two men facedown on the ground, and were in the process of tying them up. No surprise there; Ryan's men were quick thinkers. He looked over to where Maggie had been, expecting to see her lying facedown with her hands covering her head, but the spot was empty. She was gone!

"Maggie!"

He scanned the yard for a sign of her, then dismounted when he couldn't see her.

"Over here."

He followed the sound of her voice and found her by the south side of the barn, straddling the third man's back, the muzzle of a rifle leaning against the back of the man's head.

She was safe!

Relief washed over him. He called out to her, making his way to her side.

"Need any rope?" Reilly called out, walking toward them with a length of rope in his hands.

She shook her head no. "I suppose I could tie him up instead of putting a hole through him," she said, as if considering the alternative.

"Don't shoot!" the man pleaded.

Joshua stood over the man he thought was the leader and nudged him with the toe of his boot. The man moaned. "Good, you're alive. I'll need some answers," he said quietly. "Now."

The man opened his eyes. Joshua watched the man's eyes narrow, then close, and he knew the man had seen the badge he wore on his chest.

"Stay with me, friend," Joshua warned.

"I'm not going anywhere."

"Can you handle things here, Reilly?" he called out,

heading for his horse. When Reilly answered, he looked back at the man Maggie had captured. "No, but I am."

Ryan's men had all five gunmen tied up. He was going into town after Ryan.

"Aye, you and Masterson go help Jamie," he answered.

"Keep an eye on Maggie," Joshua called out, wheeling his horse to follow behind Masterson. "I've got a few more things to clear up."

"Be careful!" Maggie called out again, handing the rifle over to Mick. "Thanks for bringin' me the gun, lad."

"Me ma sent me out to help," he said, grinning up at her. "She ate all of the broth you sent up."

"Did she now?"

"Aye, and she asked when Mr. Ryan was expected back."

"Faith, she's a bold one."

"Who?" Reilly asked, coming up behind her.

"Bridget," she whispered, watching Mick walk over toward the captured gunmen.

"Mrs. O'Toole?"

"Aye, she wanted to know when Jamie'd be back."

"It's about time," Reilly said, smiling. "Himself needs a good woman."

"Aye, that he does," Maggie said with a grin, which then faded. "Do ye think they'll catch up to Jamie in time?" she asked worriedly.

"Masterson knows the trails around here like the back of his hand. They'll get there," Reilly assured her.

"Lord willing," she prayed.

"And the creek don't rise," Reilly finished for her.

"I've the proof that the ranch is mine," Ryan announced from the doorway to Hugh Emerson's private office.

"Ryan?"

"Surprised to see me?" he asked, leaning against the door jamb.

Emerson leaned forward over his desk. Ryan wondered what the man's problem was. His stomach was leaning against the blotter on his desk. The faint scraping sound of wood against wood triggered a warning in his brain. He let his hand fall to his side, and freed the loop holding his gun in the holster.

Emerson sat up with a jerk, revealing that his right hand held a derringer. The small but deadly accurate gun was pointed at Ryan's heart. "I'll take those papers," he bit out.

"You tried to take my land by force, then tried to ruin me," Ryan said quietly, not willing to risk moving and startling the overweight banker into shooting him.

"As soon as you hand over those papers, I will have accomplished my goal."

"Getting your filthy hands on me land?"

"Don't be absurd. Your ranch is one of many that I will have managed to acquire before the railroad agents start scouting out land for the new spur."

"Ye don't know for sure that they'll be wanting to run tracks through my land."

"I have a pretty fair idea that they'd be interested," Emerson said, steadying his gun hand with the other. "Too bad my man shot the wrong woman on the stage."

"You shot—"

"I had to ensure that you wouldn't get your hands on those papers."

"But you failed," Ryan said smugly. "Maggie wasn't injured."

Emerson smiled. "By the time you make it back to the ranch, she'll be dead and not one scorched stone of your house or barns will be left standing."

"If you hurt one hair on me sister's head . . ."

"Emerson!" a deep voice called out from behind Ryan, before he felt himself pushed out of the way.

He heard Emerson's derringer go off and the marshal groan, a full heartbeat before he heard the marshal's Peacemaker fire in response.

"Turner!" he said, coming to his feet to stand beside the marshal.

"Don't worry about me," Joshua bit out. "Don't let him get away!" He handed Ryan his cuffs and nodded toward Emerson.

Ryan started to knock the gun out of Emerson's hand, when he noticed that the back of the man's hand had been grazed by the marshal's bullet. Emerson stared down at his hand, moaning in agony, in too much pain to even let go of the gun still clutched in his hand.

Once Emerson was cuffed, Ryan turned back toward Joshua.

"How bad were you hit?" he asked, noticing the way the marshal held his left arm immobile.

"Not too bad," he said through clenched teeth. "But I think the bullet may have to be dug out."

Chapter Sixteen

"Why aren't they back yet?" Maggie asked for the hundredth time, pacing the kitchen floor.

"You'll wear a hole in the floor if ye don't stop," Reilly warned.

"How can you sit so calmly when Joshua and Jamie—"

The sound of horses coming up the lane had her racing out the door, flying down the porch steps.

"Joshua?" she called out, searching his face to make certain he was all right. The flash of pain that he tried to hide didn't slip past her.

"Ye've been hurt!" she accused. "Didn't I tell ye to be careful?"

"You did," he said, slowly dismounting, "and I was."

Maggie noticed how badly his left arm shook. "Were ye shot then?"

181

"Give the man a chance to explain," Ryan said sternly, tying the reins to his horse on the top rail of the corral.

"Are ye leavin' then?" she asked, noticing that he didn't put his horse in the corral.

"I have to fetch the doctor to dig a slug out of your marshal friend."

Maggie felt her stomach flip and start to revolt at the mention of a bullet piercing Joshua's flesh.

"Saints preserve—"

"I'd have done it myself," Joshua said, coming to stand beside her, "but I can't reach around the back of my shoulder."

"Come into the house." Maggie put her arm around Joshua and helped him walk across the yard.

"What, no welcome for your brother?" Ryan called out.

"*I'm* glad yer home, Jamie," a soft voice called out to him.

Maggie bit her lip to keep from laughing out loud. The way her brother's jaw dropped open was worth the price of a ticket. It was obvious he hadn't seen Bridget in the last few days. Bridget's fever was gone and her color had returned. Though still rail-thin, there was no mistaking her beauty, or the look of longing in her eyes as she stared at James.

"Did your brother know how she felt about him?" Joshua asked, leaning heavily on Maggie.

"He will," she said brightly. "Let's have a look at yer wound. Then we'll see if we need a doctor, or if I can remove it meself."

"How many bullets have you taken out?"

"None," she said, smiling at the way his face paled. He tried so hard to be strong, but she wasn't having any of it. She caught him before he stumbled.

"Don't worry, Jamie sent Reilly off the moment yer

foot touched the ground. I expect the doctor'll be back within the hour."

"Maggie, there's something I need to ask you."

"There's time enough for that once the doctor's tended yer wound."

"It can't wait."

She turned toward the man she'd given her heart to and smiled. "All right then. At least sit down so ye don't bleed all over me clean floor."

"Have a bit of sympathy for the man," her brother said, coming in the door behind them.

Maggie helped settle Joshua into a chair and began to strip away the bandages. "Mick, be a good lad and fetch me sewing basket."

Joshua surged to his feet, "Maggie, I don't think—"

Maggie caught Joshua before his knees buckled, "Ida said ye weren't partial to stitching," she said, shaking her head.

James placed a shot of whiskey on the table. Maggie picked it up and placed it in Joshua's right hand. He didn't apologize for his weakness; instead, he downed the shot in one gulp and set his glass next to the bottle for another.

"Now if ye couldn't hold yer whiskey, then I'd have something to say about it," Ryan said with a grin. "But a man who's just taken a bullet is entitled to get a bit weak in the knees."

Two hours later, the doctor had gone and Joshua was back in the kitchen.

"Are ye sure ye should be up and about?" Maggie asked, eyeing him closely, looking for signs of weakness.

"I've something to say that can't wait. Sit down, Maggie."

She started to huff at his authoritative tone then shrugged and sat.

"Maggie, you must know how I feel about you."

"Aye."

"Well?"

"Well, what?" she asked, watching his face for a clue as to what he was trying to say.

"I love you, Maggie. I have from the moment I set eyes on you."

"Joshua," she whispered, her hands moving to her lips to keep from saying the words back to him.

"Was I wrong, don't you have feelings for me?" he asked, a look of hurt flitting across his handsome features.

"No, ye weren't wrong, but ye must understand—"

"Do you love me?" he asked, interrupting.

"Aye, but I don't want to," she said, her heart breaking all over again.

"I don't understand," he said rising to his feet.

"I was pledged to marry Rory Muldoon," Maggie said in even tones, striving to hold back the tears that threatened to fall. "He died in me arms."

"Maggie . . . I didn't know—"

"How could ye? It was nigh on six years ago."

"But you'd have been too young to marry."

"I would have been sixteen the day we were to wed, if he hadn't caught the pneumonia."

Joshua rose and knelt down in front of Maggie's chair. "If I could take away the pain, I would. But I can't change the past any more than I can stop loving you. Marry me."

"I wish I could say yes," she whispered, "but look at ye!" She rose to her feet. "Ye've been shot and from what ye've said, it's not the first time."

"It comes with the territory," he said, rising to his feet to stand beside her.

"I can't marry ye. I couldn't stand not knowing when or if ye were coming back to me," she said, touching her fingertips to his lovely mouth. Unable to stop herself, she ran the tip of her forefinger along the edge of his bottom lip. His eyes darkened, and she heard his sharp intake of breath.

Maggie's heart ached. She loved him so much, it hurt. But she couldn't watch another man she loved die.

Joshua surprised her by pulling her into his arms. His lips touched hers gently at first. Her eyes closed as he increased the intensity of the kiss. His lips became more demanding as he poured every ounce of his love for her into the kiss.

He nearly broke the kiss to shout for joy, when her knees gave way. Instead, he swept her up into his arms. Shards of pain sliced through his shoulder, but he ignored it. Maggie was his. He'd die before he let her go.

"Joshua, I—"

". . . love you and want to marry you," he said, capturing her chin in his hand, not letting her look away from him.

"Don't be puttin' words in me mouth. I—"

". . . trust you and have from the moment you pulled the arrow from my arm," he said, pressing his lips gently to hers.

"Joshua, I—"

". . . can't live without you," he said, smiling, pressing a quick kiss on her brow, and then one on the tip of her nose.

"You're not listening," she wailed.

"I will when you start to make sense. I turned in my resignation a few days ago." He watched her face intently.

"Now why would ye do a thing like that?"

"Because I've had my eye on a piece of land on the other side of the river from here." He definitely liked the way her eyes softened when she was about to smile.

He kissed the corners of her mouth as she started to smile. "What would ye be raisin' on that bit of land?" she asked quietly.

"I'm after raising a few head of cattle and a passel of kids." When he captured her lips in a bone-melting kiss, all the pain of the past seemed to sort itself out. Visions of a future with Maggie filled him with contentment.

Maggie knew she'd have to say yes, when he kissed her the first time. Heaven help her, she didn't want to, but how else could he play a part in her future if she let him walk away? Long-dead dreams of a home and family resurfaced. She knew now that what she'd felt for Rory would always have a special place in her heart and memories, but what she felt for Joshua would carry them through the rest of their lives.

She wanted to tend the land alongside of him, raising cattle, and babies with green eyes and sun-kissed hair. She'd be a fool to pass up the gift of love he was holding out to her. It was hers for the taking; all she had to do was reach out with with an open mind and loving heart.

She wrapped her arms around his neck and pulled him against her, until not a breath of air was left between them. She raised her lips and whispered, "Just how many kids are in a passel?"